THE ENDING LEGACY

LINDSEY POGUE
LINDSEY SPARKS

Editing by Holly Hill Mangin
Fresh as a Daisy Editing
Proofreading by Nicole Hartney
Letter-Eye Editing
Cover Design by Deranged Doctor Designs

L2 Books
101 W. American Canyon Rd. Ste. 508-262
American Canyon, CA 94503

978-1949485264

THE ENDING WORLD

Maryland: Dr. Anna Cartwright discovers a base pair on a specific strand of DNA estimated to be present in a little over 10 percent of the human population. It holds the genetic key to accessing never-before-seen mental and physical abilities. She reads an article about gene therapy and sets out to conduct human trials.

1978

In a second round of trials, Dr. Anna Cartwright's collegue, Gregory Herodson, asks her to administer the gene therapy to him. Once developed, Herodson begins honing his Ability, using Anna to amplify it, and starts putting his plan and mind-controlled army into place for the Great Transformation.

1988

Colorado Springs: Gregory Herodson, now a General, takes Anna away from her family, threatening the lives of her family if she ever disobeys him. Anna changes her name to Dr. Wesley, and becomes the General's plaything and greatest weapon.

Nevada: PANBO BIOTECH implements the Fulfillment Study (also known as the Program), which attracts candidates through solicitation and then alters their DNA. If the subject carries the Pandora strand they develop special abilities, if they don't carry the strand they get very sick and either go mad or die.

1990

The Colony: General Herodson makes Dr. Wesley create a modified influenza virus, nearly universally contagious and designed to take advantage of the weakened immune systems of the non-P-strand carriers. They release the Virus on the general population.

2012

United States: People begin getting sick with an unknown flu that is spreading rapidly, deaths are being reported. The Center for Disease Control start quarantining people based on whether or not they've had H1N1.

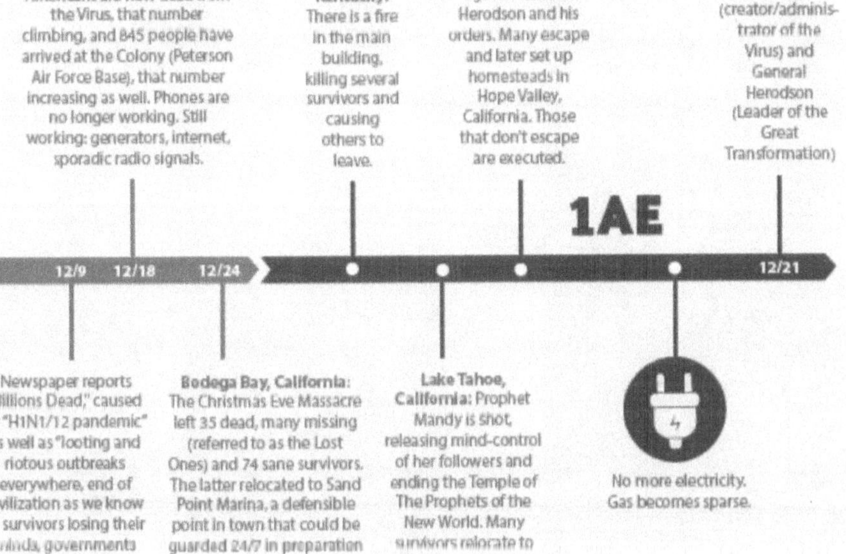

A new report comes over the radio that says 87% of Americans are now dead from the Virus, that number climbing, and 845 people have arrived at the Colony (Peterson Air Force Base), that number increasing as well. Phones are no longer working. Still working: generators, internet, sporadic radio signals.

Fort Knox Military Base, Kentucky: There is a fire in the main building, killing several survivors and causing others to leave.

The Colony: Re-gens rebel against General Herodson and his orders. Many escape and later set up homesteads in Hope Valley, California. Those that don't escape are executed.

Petaluma, California: Anna Cartwright (creator/administrator of the Virus) and General Herodson (Leader of the Great Transformation)

1AE

12/9   12/18   12/24

12/21

Newspaper reports "Billions Dead," caused by "H1N1/12 pandemic" as well as "looting and riotous outbreaks everywhere, end of civilization as we know it, survivors losing their minds, governments can't control, the Apocalypse."

Bodega Bay, California: The Christmas Eve Massacre left 35 dead, many missing (referred to as the Lost Ones) and 74 sane survivors. The latter relocated to Sand Point Marina, a defensible point in town that could be guarded 24/7 in preparation for the return of the 107 Lost Ones.

Lake Tahoe, California: Prophet Mandy is shot, releasing mind-control of her followers and ending the Temple of The Prophets of the New World. Many survivors relocate to Zephyr Cove, a nearby campground.

No more electricity. Gas becomes sparse.

PROLOGUE

285AE

Campfire smoke drifted through the crisp morning air, and the livestock began to stir in their pens. Soon, the village would be bustling, marking the start of another day that would meld into the next, until it was no longer worth keeping track.

Usually, I craved the predawn quiet, but with every briny breeze and wave crashing beyond the forest cliffs, I thought of *them*. It felt like a lifetime ago, and if I let the sound of the distant waterfalls fill my ears, I thought of her and of *us*. This was the life she'd wanted, simple and hidden away with nothing but the Old California coast stretching out for miles each way. Even if the memories felt hazy as the years continued to pass, I still ached every time I remembered life from . . . *before*.

With a reluctant sigh, I pushed the memories away and peered through the ferns and redwoods, deeper into the forest. These people were my concern now—my promise—not the ghosts of the past, and the longer the forest remained silent around me, the tighter the tension coiled in my gut.

The hunting party was two days late returning, and while Fin and Beast were the best hunters we had, Fin was also only nineteen, and he was our most impulsive and stubborn hunter, too. I hoped he hadn't decided to go off course. Like most of the villagers, he lived a sheltered life in the thick of the trees, where the Pacific Ocean met the towering redwoods jutting from the cliffs.

To Fin and everyone else who lived in the village, Herodson, the dangers of nearby Corvo City, and even the Corvo queen were little more than watered-down cautionary tales that spanned the centuries—musings of power-hungry manipulators that shaped the decaying world into the rural, lonely, and haunted place it had become.

Fin hadn't lived through war and famine, and his heart wasn't hardened by the loss of everyone he held dear. Even his parents were less than a dull memory, dead too soon after he was born. While Fin and the other villagers were eager to learn and welcomed my teachings, Fin had no idea how important our history would be one day. To him. To his sister. To his people.

The cabin door opened, and Autumn poked her head out. Her blonde hair hung long and curly around her shoulders, mussed from sleep. Her green eyes shone brightly in the overcast sunlight, and I looked at the glowing embers of the fire to avert my gaze.

A rooster crowed somewhere down the lane, and Autumn came over to warm her hands to the flames across from me. "You never came in last night," she said quietly, her tone almost careful. We had many unspoken agreements, and not talking about *us*, whatever we were, was one of them. "You're worried about Fin," she added. "But you've taught him well, J. He's okay—"

"How do you know?" My gaze cut to hers, and the knot in my gut tightened.

Autumn's expression, always a little reserved when it came to me, softened. "I can feel it."

"Then where the hell are they?" I grumbled.

Her shoulders straightened at my tone, and I stared back into the morning fire.

"Sorry," I said and tossed another log onto the flames. "You didn't deserve that." Autumn deserved a lot more than anything I could ever give her.

I pulled the kettle off the rack and poured her a cup of hot water for her tea. With a tight-lipped smile, she reached for the mug and held it in her hands to warm them.

My frown slid back into place, and I scrubbed my hands over my face, exhaling an anxious breath.

"Promise me you'll keep them safe." Words from another life echoed like a distant heartbeat, always present and everlasting. I couldn't fail them. I couldn't fail *her*.

"You should go," Autumn whispered. "You know you won't feel better until you do, and if anyone can track them, it's you." I didn't deserve the patience in her voice. She nodded toward the cabin. "I readied your pack last night, just in case," she added, and this time I met her gaze. I didn't deserve her kindness, either. Despite the carefully constructed walls between us, it felt like she knew me better than I knew myself sometimes.

Wrapping her shawl tighter around her shoulders, Autumn turned for the cabin, her mug clutched in one hand, and I rose to my feet. She was right, she was always right. I needed to find Fin and the hunting party because, after a lifetime of running, all I could ever do was worry.

I met her at the door as she stepped out again with my pack hanging at her side. "I put in some meat and bread for you," she said, handing it to me, her muscles straining.

With a nod of thanks, I slung the pack over my shoulder, then reached for my bow and quiver resting beside the door.

"Your pack should have everything you need for tracking and in case it rains," she added a bit uneasily; her eyes were fixed on my pack as she licked her lips. "You have water, and I even put some—"

"Autumn." Her name was nearly a whisper as I willed her to meet my gaze. I wanted her to see what I couldn't bring myself to say. *You deserve a whole man who can love you the way you should be loved.*

Finally, her green eyes that held too much hope and too much forgiveness shifted to mine.

"Thank you," I said instead.

She blinked and dipped her chin with a steadying sigh. "You're welcome." Despite the dozens of reasons why I could never give her what she wanted or deserved, she was always there, unbearably gracious and understanding. She cleared her throat. "You should go before the winds pick up again and compromises their trail more than it already is." With a forced smile, she turned to the door. "Be safe—"

"Hey." I reached for her arm.

Autumn's eyes shimmered in the overcast morning as her gaze trailed from my hand up to my face.

I leaned in and pressed a kiss to her lips, offering her all that I could. "Take care of everyone for me until I get back."

Slowly, her eyes flitted open and she inhaled a steadying breath. "Just bring my little brother back to me, Jake."

With a nod and a final glance at the village, I turned and headed into the forest, determined to find Fin.

The pack grew heavier on my back as I weaved around the redwoods that towered over me, following the path of broken ferns toward Fallen Wood, where the trees were upturned and their roots were exposed and outreaching, like giant witch fingers in a foggy forest. It was a graveyard of giants and provided ample places to hide if Fin and the hunters had needed to do so.

But a nagging voice told me that if they were still alive, I would know for certain. Beast would've returned home, at least, or Claire would have sent a telepathic message letting us know they would be gone longer. Then again, she would've warned us if something had gone wrong, too.

I often wondered if I would regret establishing the descendant community here. In my heart, it was the only place I'd ever considered home—the only place that felt right. And as the Corvo kingdom continued to expand, it was easy enough to ignore the possible dangers because I'd convinced myself that the vast, Feral-ridden, ancient woods would protect us and the descendants' strong, multifaceted Abilities would keep them safe. Now, I worried I had made a grave mistake.

For four hours I'd been tracking Fin's carefully covered steps, only identifiable by the occasional broken fern or matted leaves. Gripping my bow tightly in one hand, I crouched down to inspect the tracks more closely. There were no footprints or discarded debris. They'd done as they were taught, and as far as I could tell, I'd been the only one to follow after them. From this direction, at least.

As their trail led me closer to the felled giants in the clearing, I heard the caw of ravens and saw a flutter through the trees, then a familiar gray and red tunic. Lifting my bow with unease, I moved closer, eyeing the muddy footprints and listening to the rustling conifers above.

The ravens dispersed as I stepped through the ferns. I spotted Timmons's body in a bloody heap first. His eyes were open, and his mouth was agape. He'd been dead for a handful of hours, at least.

Heart racing, I scoured the forest floor, noticing four more bodies spread out between the trees. I ran to each of them, checking their pulses out of desperation, though it was clear they'd been dead through the night.

Claire. Bud. Chuck. Dallace. All of them had a hole seared through their chests. Not the result of a Feral ambush with knives and spears. The wounds were too sophisticated, too precise for a horde of Crazies, and the footprints in the moist earth were thick-soled and uniform, every tread matching the next. These innocent hunters were killed by well-trained, Ability-wielding soldiers that were too far from Corvo City to have been here for any reason other than one: they were looking for something.

I suppressed the urge to call for Fin as I rose to my feet, my gaze darting through the trees. A predatory yowl echoed, and I spun around. A cougar stood on the top of a boulder, his tail lashing anxiously behind him.

"Beast," I rasped, and another wave of dread washed over me. "Where is he?"

The cougar's ears laid back and he lifted his muzzle to the air, as if he were sniffing for danger, and yowled again. Eventually, he turned for me to follow him.

My bootsteps were heavy, crunching over twigs as I hurried around the upturned roots toward the mass of boulders at the clearing's edge. Beast jumped down from one boulder to the next, until he landed on the ground with a thud, and trotted toward a thicket that butted up to the boulder's base.

Fin was crumpled in the brush. His tan tunic was dirty and torn, but unlike the others, he wasn't covered in blood, and there was no hole in his chest. Only cuts and bruises darkened his face and hands, and I dropped to my knees beside him.

"Fin," I choked. My pack fell to the ground with a thunk. He was unconscious, but he was alive. "Fin," I snapped more urgently.

Beast paced behind me, his tail still lashing through the air as he growled with unease.

"Fin," I bit out and shook him awake. "Wake up, damn it."

Slowly, his eyelids flitted open, and my breath caught in my throat. His eyes were the same brilliant green as his sister's, and I allowed myself a sigh of relief.

"What happened?" I asked, my voice low and calmer as the panic subsided a little.

He blinked. "What—" His eyes rounded as his memories fell back into place, and he nearly shot to his feet. "They were here—the rangers." Horror filled Fin's eyes. "They had a Null with them, stronger than me. I couldn't detect their Abilities until . . ." He shook his head in disbelief. "They surrounded us. They got Dallace first, and then—"

"Slow down, Fin," I told him. "Take a breath."

But Fin was running toward Claire's body before I could stop him. "No," he murmured, stumbling the last few steps. "We weren't doing anything wrong." His voice cracked as he knelt beside his best friend's body. "They didn't have to hurt us. We were just hunting, we were on the trail like you said. I was going to go a different way, but you told me not to . . . I just—"

"I know, kid," I said, crouching down beside him. I gripped his shoulder and made him look at me. "This is what they do. It's what they've *always* done." But not for sport. There was always a reason for the queen's rangers to seek us out, rational or not. "What did they want, Fin? What were they looking for?" The village, a hundred people strong, was in danger.

His eyes welled with tears as he glanced from one fallen friend to the next. "Who."

The crease in my brow deepened. "What?"

Fin blinked at me, bleary-eyed. "Not *what* they were looking for," he said more forcefully. "*Who.*"

I leaned back as his words sank in. I knew the answer before he said it.

"You, Jake . . . They were looking for *you*."

Blood-boiling hatred and white-knuckled fear flooded through me at once. "And you're alive because they have a message," I finished for him.

Fin nodded as a vacant expression filled his face, like he was still trying to catch up to all that had happened. Or maybe he was finally starting to understand everything I'd been trying to explain all of these years.

Finally, Fin rose to his feet and stared down at me with uncertainty. "They want you to go to Corvo City, or they'll return and kill us all."

It was only a matter of time before something like this happened again. Jaw set, I rose to my feet. I'd become too complacent; I should've been prepared for this.

"They know where the village is," Fin continued. "They know we're the descendants of their *Patrons*, and they know who you are and that you're here. This was only a warning."

I stared at him as my breath seized in my lungs and her familiar, haunting voice filled my head again. *"Promise me you'll keep them safe."* I glanced from Claire's body to the bodies of Dallace and Timmons, imagining the look on their families' faces when Fin returned with the news.

We'd been able to live in peace for years, on the periphery of a world I barely recognized anymore, but our years of feeling a false sense of security near the outskirts of a corrupt kingdom were gone. The Corvo queen had found us, and I knew all too well that her soldiers would keep to their word if I didn't give her what she wanted.

"Run back to the village, Fin," I told him as my legs moved with deadly purpose. I gathered Claire's body into my arms and carried her over to the protection of the brush around the boulder where their remains would be safe there until Autumn and Fin could return for them. "I'll hide their bodies for now.

Tell your sister what's happened, and be quick and quiet about it —I don't want everyone seeing them like this."

Fin listened with rapt attention. His fingers ticked at his sides, and I could see the whirlwind of questions and fear in his eyes. But he pushed the questions away, along with his tears, and nodded.

"Beast stays here to keep the animals away until you return. Bring the wagon to collect their bodies, then take them home to their families. Go on, now," I commanded, and strode over to Dallace.

Fin turned to leave, then froze, and his head snapped to me. "What are you going to do?"

I didn't look at him as I lugged Dallace's muscular frame into the brush to lay beside Claire.

"What I have to do."

Fin stomped over to me. "What's that mean, Jake?" he demanded. The authority in his voice was admirable, and I was proud, even.

"It means, I'm turning myself in," I admitted.

"They'll just keep coming for us, whether you turn yourself in or not."

"No, they won't," I told him with certainty.

"You said yourself, we can't trust them." I could hear his frantic footsteps behind me as I headed toward Timmons's cold, dead body.

"They want me. Not you." If nothing else, I could learn what exactly it was they wanted. They knew the location of our village, but they hadn't attacked and killed us all in our sleep. There had to be a reason.

"You don't know that for sure," Fin argued. "What if they come back for us anyway?"

There were three more hunter's bodies to find; eight innocent people to bury because of me, and they would be the last. I would make damn sure of that.

"Jake—"

"It has to be done, kid," I barked out.

"But if you give them what they want, we'll have no leverage against them."

I whipped around to face him. "And if I do nothing, they will kill all of you for certain. Sorry, Fin, but I won't have that on my conscience. No more death, not because of me."

"But . . . what about Autumn? What about your life here—we might never see you again."

"Your sister wants you safe," I told him. "And this is the only way that's going to happen. She'll agree with this decision. Now get the hell out of here so your friends can be laid to rest. Go, Fin."

"Jake—"

"Now!" I shouted. My chest heaved and my heart ached as I realized he was right about one thing—this might be the last time I ever saw him. It would likely be the last time I ever stepped foot in this forest again.

Fin's eyes narrowed, and he lifted his chin defiantly. He was a good kid—a good man—great even, but he was stubborn, and I saw the wheels turning behind those expressive eyes of his.

"It's the only option," I told him more calmly. "I'm not watching all of you die because of me. No more will be said about it."

Fin's nostrils flared and he squared his shoulders, his hands balling into fists at his sides. Then, finally, he forced himself to walk away.

"Fin," I growled.

He paused but didn't look back at me. "Take care of your sister for me."

My heart was a sledgehammer in my chest as I waited for him to say something, something that meant he didn't hate me, or at least that he wouldn't hate me forever. The last thing I wanted was to leave him, the way so many of the people in his life had, but I had no choice.

I worried his acknowledgment wouldn't come until, finally, he said, "I will." He stalked into the trees without bothering to look back.

I

DEL

Nerves fluttering, I held my breath as I pulled the heavy door to the vault open on silent hinges. I exhaled my relief, grateful I hadn't disturbed the quiet of the sleeping castle with my midnight sneaking. It probably wouldn't look good for the crown princess to be caught snooping around her mother's vault in the middle of the night.

The whispers I had been hearing for months grew louder as the door opened, convincing me that I was on the right track, and renewed determination overrode any nervousness about being here. Mother had long ago forbidden me from entering this vault, but I couldn't resist any longer. Not when I could sense she was hiding something from me—something terrible. And certainly not with the whispers interfering with my daily life; much longer, and I feared they would drive me insane.

As I moved into the open doorway, the soft orange light emanating from the electric torch in my hand spilled into the vault, illuminating a cluttered space filled with a hodgepodge of crates, chests, and other storage containers. The stone walls and floor appeared golden in the warm light, and the air had a dank, musty quality that made me wrinkle my nose.

Sid stirred on my shoulder, the raven anxiously ruffling his feathers.

"Go on, look around," I said, glancing at him sidelong. "I know you want to."

With a muted caw and another ruffle of feathers, Sid launched himself into the air, his talons digging into the leather lining the shoulder of my robe before releasing. I tilted my head away from him, but it was never truly possible to avoid the brush of his onyx wings. I watched him soar around the vault, appreciating the graceful swerve and sway of his flight.

Obsidian—Sid, as I called him—and I couldn't actually speak to one another, at least, not in the same way some Telepaths could communicate with nonhuman creatures, but we understood each other well enough. As a raven, he was one of the few types of birds that could mimic human speech, which helped. He had been my companion since birth, when he was little more than a fledgling; such was the tradition in my family, established nearly two centuries ago, with the dawn of the Corvo dynasty. Over the eighteen years that Sid and I had been together, we had developed our own form of communication.

I supposed my Ability helped. I belonged in the Empath Class, as had all crown princesses and queens of the Corvo dynasty before me. Whereas Mother was a strong, but common Direct Empath, her gifts allowing her to glean thoughts and memories from any human within her sight, I was a rarer Resonant Empath, my gifts triggered by touch and centered around memories, though I could sense another's surface thoughts and emotions as well, so long as my skin was touching theirs. The only upside to the way my Ability had manifested was that it wasn't limited to humans; I could pick up memories—or *resonances*—from both nonhuman creatures and from certain objects. It didn't enable me to communicate with Sid telepathically, but it did allow me to see the world as he saw it, through his memories. It helped me understand him and come up with new ways to help him understand me.

I watched Sid make one more circuit around the vault before landing on a stack of crates near the center of the room. He fluffed his feathers as he settled his wings, and then he started preening.

Smirking, I shook my head and turned away from him. Silly bird. I reached for the door handle and pulled it toward me, easing the heavy door shut. Electric torch held out in front of me, I cautiously wound through the room, following the lure of the whispers. They stemmed from a resonance—the strongest I had ever felt. It lingered longer than any had before, almost seeming to have a mind of its own.

The vault wasn't nearly as grand or mysterious as I imagined, more like a glorified storage room than the trove of treasures I constructed in my mind. I walked past stacks of wooden crates, mixed with chests and trunks of every imaginable style, from antique to modern, from leather to wood to metal. Steamer trunks had been stored beside hope chests, museum crates beside rusted footlockers; the only similarity shared between them was the thick layer of dust coating their lids.

The whispers led me to the back corner of the vault, to where a carved wooden chest, with dings born of countless years of use, lay buried under three smaller crates. I touched each crate in turn, then brushed my fingertips along the top of the chest.

Instantly, the whispers increased in volume and fervor, excited by the contact. This was it—what they wanted me to find.

I pulled my hand away and eyed the crates resting atop the chest. They weren't large. I only hoped that translated into them not being heavy, either.

I set the electric torch on a nearby steamer trunk, then reached up to the top crate and pulled it from the stack to set it on the floor beside the wooden chest. I moved the middle crate just as easily, but the bottom one proved to be too heavy to lift, so I slid it to the edge of the chest and, groaning with effort, lowered it to the floor. My grip slipped at the last second, and the crate hit the floor with a resounding thud and the crack of wood.

I crouched there for long seconds, staring at the crate. The wood panel on one side had split, and the frame at the base had popped free.

"Uh oh!" Sid exclaimed, his croaking voice ripping through the stillness of the room.

I cringed, glancing back at the raven who was watching me with one beady, black eye. "Hopefully nobody will notice that," I muttered, biting my bottom lip.

Sid cawed, then extended his wings and hopped off his perch, gliding down to the damaged crate. His talons clacked on the wooden top as he strutted around, adjusting his wings.

The whispers drew my attention back to the chest. Two small patches on the edge of the lid had been cleared of dust, as though someone had recently been here and opened it.

That *someone* was Mother. It had to be. The whispers had started when I not-so-accidentally brushed my hand against hers in an attempt to figure out exactly what she was hiding from me. She may have been able to shield her mind from me, but with that brief contact, she had unintentionally passed on the remnants of something ancient. A resonance she couldn't sense.

I knelt on the floor in front of the chest and pressed the heels of my hands against the edge of the lid. It barely budged with my first attempt to lift it, and I wondered if the humid bay air had warped the wood over the years. There was no saying just how old the chest was—just that it looked ancient.

Pressing my lips together, I pushed the lid up with all my might, a sharp grunt escaping from my throat. The lid creaked and groaned, slowly inching upward.

And then, suddenly, it was free. I coughed and waved away a cloud of dust as the whispers grew louder, beckoning me onward.

Sid hopped closer, then jumped from the crate to the rim of the open chest.

I reached for the electric torch and angled the warm, orange light into the chest, revealing a wide assortment of items, all worn by age. I pulled out a cloth bundle, layers of fragile, soft fabric wound around something hard, and carefully started to unwrap whatever was within. I thought the cloth may have been a beautiful scarf, once upon a time, but the fine fabric was littered with tears and moth-holes, and it had been so discolored by age that the pattern was indiscernible. Images flitted through my mind, resonances too wispy and indistinct to make out.

When I reached the hardness at the center of the bundle, I unveiled a tiny cat curled in sleep, carved from wood and polished until it was smooth as silk. I held the figurine on my palm and closed my eyes, waiting for a resonance that never came. Like the scarf, the figurine wasn't the source of the beckoning whispers. I set both aside on the floor and reached into the chest for the next item.

An intricately carved wooden box, square, all four sides about the length of my forearm, but half as tall. Something shifted within the box, rustling softly, as though it contained pieces of paper. I lifted the hinged lid, revealing a mass of faded, crumbling photographs, their images indiscernible.

Sid crept closer along the rim of the chest, and I leaned in over the smaller box, wondering if the photographs could be salvaged and their images revealed. But opening the box hadn't excited the whispers, and only the ghosts of memories danced around the edges of my mind as I peered down at the photographs. This wasn't the source of the resonance, either, which meant I needed to move on.

I shut the box and set it aside, then reached into the chest, pulling out a pocket knife, the worn wooden handle cracked and darkened by age. When the knife didn't trigger any memories, I set it aside, too, before returning to the chest.

The next item was a book, the brown leather cover pressed with a symbol I knew all too well. A knot that had always reminded me of a tangled heart. It was the symbol stamped onto the cover of The Book, printed and distributed on Mother's orders to every household within the kingdom's borders. The Book was broken into two parts. The second half, called *The World After*, chronicled the history of the Corvo kingdom and the world that had existed before the chaos that birthed the order that now ruled our daily lives. The first part, called *The World Before*, read less like a history book and more like a novel, describing the lives and times of the Patrons—originals who, according to legend, had risen to an elite, idolized status because of their notable actions during the Turn—and imparting the Patrons' wisdom to the reader through shorter parables.

What did it mean that this symbol was here, on *this* book? Was it possible that this was the original source of *The World Before*?

I reached for the aged book, and the instant my fingertips touched the soft leather, the whispers stopped. I closed my eyes, bowed my head, and took long, soothing deep breaths, basking in the sudden silence. The quiet felt foreign and exotic. It had been so long since I'd been alone in my head—so very long—and I felt slightly unbalanced in the absence of the hum.

When I opened my eyes, a small smile curved my lips. This was it—the thing I had come here for. The thing I had defied Mother's orders for. The thing that had nearly driven me insane.

Gingerly, almost reverently, I traced the depression carved by the symbol on the cover of the book with my fingertip. This was hers. Zoe's. I could feel it.

Zoe was the Patron of my Ability Class, the original Empath.

The Telepaths had Dani. The Gauges had Jason. The Elementals, Carlos. The Supers, Mase. The Oracles, Becca. The Sensors, Sam. The Movers, Camille. The Healers had Jake, but their Class was so rare that it was believed to be nearly extinct. And then there was the one whose name we never uttered, save for in hushed tones behind closed doors. Herodson, the demon Patron of the forbidden Class: the Controllers. The ones who were doomed at birth, by no fault of their own other than the unfortunate appearance of recessive genes. The ones who were too dangerous to let live. It was the truth the Corvo kingdom had been founded upon—Controllers must die.

Sid hopped along the rim of the chest, his head cocking this way and that as he looked from me to the book and back. "Story time!" he croaked, hopping in place and fluffing his feathers. The silly raven loved it when I read out loud to him.

I laughed under my breath and shook my head. "Yeah, yeah," I told Sid as my fingers curled around the spine of the book. "I'll read you a story." I gently picked the book up, turning to sit with my back resting against the front of the chest.

The leather spine creaked as I lifted the cover. The first page was blank, but when I turned to the next, I was greeted by two lines of handwriting that made my heart beat faster.

Stories from the World Before
by Zoe Cartwright

There it was—confirmation that this book really was hers. It really was Zoe's—*the* Zoe. And not just her belonging, but her creation.

Mother had long claimed that the contents of *The World Before* had been pulled from an ancient text composed by the originals. I had never asked her for proof, but part of me always suspected her claim was merely a clever bit of propaganda. Mother was nothing if not clever. She had to be to hold the kingdom together for so long.

Heart racing, I turned the page, admiring the compact lines of neat handwriting. *Zoe's* handwriting. I inhaled deeply, cleared my throat, and started to read the words of my Patron, written over two and a half centuries ago.

Looking backward at the past and then forward to the future, I think about how changeable life is. How two years ago I feared such trivial things, like being unable to pay my rent on time or make a car payment. Now, along with hoping for the future, I fear what I don't know—there's still so much left to learn about this new world we're living in. In many ways, I fear my Ability because there's still so much to learn about the people around me, too . . .

The words faded away as I continued to read, and flashes of memories filled my mind. Page after page, those flashes stretched out into moments. Into scenes. Into lifetimes.

I was a teenage boy, experiencing the prolonged illness and death of a much-beloved sister. I was a middle-aged man, a teacher, taking a chance on love after a heartbreaking loss. I was a young man making the difficult decision to leave my family behind and join the military. I was a mother, forced into servitude, and made to do terrible things in order to protect my family. I was a young woman, trying—and failing—to save her abused mother. I was a fierce mother of twins, experiencing the greatest heartbreak known to mankind—the death of my children. I was a couple of teenage girls, taking one last road trip together before saying goodbye and going our separate ways. I was a young man, struggling to tell the girl I loved how I felt.

In a flash, I was me again, reading Zoe's words from the aged pages of the book. Sid was perched on my shoulder, his head tucked against his wing, and his eyes were closed. Not wanting to disturb his slumber, I read on in silence.

I've seen the terrifying secret Becca has been keeping from us. I can barely fathom it, let alone find the words to describe it.

Things are changing. The future of humankind is so uncertain, tears burn my eyes. I have to write it down—get it out of me, somehow—even if I can't tell anyone. I need to find Becca so she can explain what it is I saw. I need her to explain the insanity I witnessed.

In the dream, I saw—

The sentence cut off prematurely. Brow furrowing, I turned the page, expecting to find more writing or at least an explanation for the abrupt ending to the previous section. But there was nothing. A quick search of the remaining pages revealed that the rest of the book was blank. I returned to the final entry, studying the last line.

In the dream, I saw—

Rereading Zoe's final words sent a chill cascading down my spine. I raised my eyes from the page, staring past the crates to the stone wall beyond, like it might reveal the secrets Zoe was hiding. What had she been about to write? What had she seen? *What* insanity?

I couldn't help but wonder if she had caught a glimpse of this world, as it was now. Of my world. It was so different from hers; just as her world was so different from what I had been told. I could see the similarities between Zoe's account of the world *before* and the stories in The Book. The resemblance was close enough to tell me Mother had pulled them from Zoe's journal, but she had warped the words, twisted the stories, molding the truth into something that would serve her purposes—that would promote her purist ideals and keep her people docile. That would keep her kingdom strong, the iron fist with which she ruled: unbreakable.

The Patrons weren't saints. They weren't perfect beings who foresaw a world different—better—than their own. They were just like us. They were people. Human beings. They had fears and memories and so many secrets. They were just trying to survive.

Just like me.

What would they think of us now, worshiping them like gods?

Reading about events I thought I knew so well, but in Zoe's own words, shed an entirely different light on the world during the Turn, changing my perception of the world around me. Of *my* world. A world built upon lies. Curiosity far from sated, I was more desperate than ever to uncover the truth. Why had Mother been lying to us—to me, her heir—for so long? And what else was she hiding?

Because of Zoe—of her words—I was more determined than ever to find out.

I shut the book and shifted, stretching out my legs. Sid roused, ruffling his feathers as he cawed softly. "What is Mother up to?" I murmured.

Sid angled his head away from mine and snapped his beak.

The raven was none-too-fond of Mother, and a hostile beak snap was his usual response whenever I mentioned her.

I smiled, peering at him out of the corner of my eye. "At least I know I can trust you," I told him and raised a hand to tickle his fluffed up chest, earning a contented chitter.

Turning my attention back to the leather-bound book, I leafed through the pages, settling on one in the middle of the first story, filled with a sketch rather than handwriting. Zoe had drawn a burly looking man sitting at a table, his forearms resting on the surface and his eyes filled with sympathy. How she had managed to imbue so much emotion into the sketch was beyond me. It was so lifelike, almost more realistic than a photograph.

My gift told me this was Jake, Zoe's husband, the original Healer.

Ever so lightly, I traced the lines of his face with the tip of my pointer finger. Flashes of more memories flitted through my mind's eye, resonances of moments from Zoe and Jake's life together. Happy moments. Tender moments. Painful moments. And as quickly as it started, the shuffle of memories faded away, and I was back to staring at the sketch of a man I now felt like I knew.

I had never experienced a resonance from anything so ancient as this book. I wondered if these memories were able to span the centuries because of Zoe's Ability—because she had been an Empath, like me.

A gentle chime rang out from the pendant watch hanging on a silver chain around my neck. It chimed five times, and my shoulders drooped.

"Time's up!" Sid croaked, bobbing his head like he was encouraging me to get moving.

He was right. I had set the timepiece to alert me at five in the morning. It was just under two hours until sunrise, which meant less than an hour until the servants entered my room to relight the fire in the hearth before I woke. While they probably wouldn't examine my bed closely enough to realize that the slumbering lump was really just a few pillows stuffed strategically under the covers, I wasn't willing to risk it. Not when I was finally making progress in my search for the truth.

I bent my knees and, groaning, stood up. Sid launched himself from my shoulder, flapping his onyx wings once to give himself some lift, then coasted to land atop a low stack of trunks nearby. I quickly returned the items I had removed from the chest but hesitated in returning the book.

"Surely nobody will notice this is missing," I murmured as I held the book over the open chest.

Making up my mind, I tucked the leather-bound book under my arm and reached out with my free hand to lower the lid of the chest. When the two lighter crates were stacked atop it once more, I turned my attention to the damaged one. With a few grunts, I nudged the offending crate partway behind the chest, turning it slightly to hide the damage from view.

I took a step back, brushing off my hands and assessing my work. Not perfect, but good enough. I retrieved the book from the chest and headed for the door.

Sid cawed, then croaked, "Finders keepers!" It was his way of saying I had left something behind.

I turned around in time to see him gliding down to land beside the electric torch, sitting on top of a steamer trunk. I hurried back, snatched up the electric torch, and headed for the door, skimming my fingertips over a few of the storage containers as I passed to see if I could pick up any residual resonances. Everything was too benign or insignificant, and my mind's eye remained dark.

Until my fingertips made contact with a newer looking metal case sitting on top of a short stack of crates near the door.

· · ·

I had a bird's-eye view of a room filled with stretchers, each holding a person. Some struggled against their restraints, while others were passed out cold. IVs drained blood from their arms, and red-robed individuals moved among the stretchers, changing out full blood bags for empties and depositing the full bags in a large bin of ice at the center of the room.

I jerked my hand away from the case, hissing as though I had been burned. I had no idea what I had just seen. All I knew was how it had made me feel: horrified. Who were those people, and why were they there—wherever *there* was—being held against their will as they were drained of their life's blood?

I wasn't willing to bury my head in the sand, ignoring the evidence that was right in front of me. Not any longer. I had to know what Mother was up to.

Hand shaking, I reached for the case again, guarding my mind against the disturbing resonance. I needed to find out what else the case contained besides those mental horrors. I lifted the lid and leaned closer, peering inside.

The case was filled with narrow glass vials, each tucked into an individual slot.

Taking a deep breath and holding the air in my lungs, I pinched the top of one of the vials between my thumb and fore-finger and pulled it free from the case. Through the clear glass, I could see the iridescent liquid filling the vial. I tilted it to the side, brow furrowing as I watched the viscous liquid slowly shift within.

Without warning, a resonance invaded my mind.

A man was laid out on a stretcher, strapped down as an IV drained his blood. He screamed, his body writhing and pulling against the restraints. He was so tired of this never-ending torture. He wished it would all end. Every night, he dreamed of the sweet peace of death. A sweet peace he feared he would never know.

The resonance ended in a blink, a mere flicker in my mind's eye, but it was enough to make my heart gallop and my blood run cold. The vial slipped from my grasp and smashed against the stone floor, glass shattering. I jumped backward to avoid the splatter.

"Uh oh!" Sid croaked unhelpfully, landing beside the metal case on the crate.

I gulped, my eyes widening, and licked my lips as I stared down at the mess. I had to clean it up. I couldn't leave such glaring evidence of my intrusion, but I had no idea what the liquid was. What if it was some kind of poison?

Thinking fast, I set the book and electric torch on the crate near Sid, then shrugged out of my robe and crouched near the mess. My robe was lined with a thin layer of leather to protect me from Sid's talons; I just hoped it would stand up against shards of glass and potential poison, as well.

Thankfully, I was able to clean up the spill, only a residual sheen of wetness indicating that anything had happened, but I figured that would dry. I placed my hand down on the floor beside me, intending to push up to stand, but sucked in a sharp breath when a searing pain stabbed into my palm.

As the blood drained from my face, I raised my hand and turned it over, looking down at my palm. A small shard of glass was embedded in the heel of my hand, just below the base of my thumb, and blood trickled down my wrist and forearm.

I swallowed, my mouth instantly dry. If the liquid was some kind of poison, I would know soon enough.

And then something shocking happened.

The glass was pushed out of my flesh like my body was rejecting it. My skin burned as the wound started to close up right before my eyes. The burning turned into an itching sensation that was almost worse than the pain.

But then it stopped, and all that remained of the wound was the blood.

"Oh, my God," I breathed.

Eyes wide, I wiped my hand on the front of my nightgown, the black silk concealing the crimson blood. When I looked at my palm again, the skin was perfect. No hint of the wound, not even a scar.

The liquid in the vials was no poison. Quite the opposite, in fact. It seemed to be some sort of miracle elixir. But how could such a thing exist? As wondrous as it seemed, I couldn't shake the horror of the resonance. The elixir was a creation born of terrible pain and suffering, of that I had no doubt.

But where was this happening? And how? Why? There were still so many questions. Too many questions. I needed to find out more before I confronted Mother about the horrifying truth.

Flustered by my discovery, I picked up the stray piece of glass, tucked it into the safety of the bundled up robe, and stood. I held out my forearm for Sid, and as he climbed up to my shoulder, his talons digging painfully into my skin, I shut the metal case. After retrieving the leather-bound book and the electric torch, I rushed to the door. I gave the vault one final scan, making sure nothing looked overtly out of place, then pushed the heavy door open and slipped out into the dark hallway before turning to case the door shut.

"Go, Sid," I said, craning my neck to peer at the raven on my shoulder. "Scout ahead. Make sure the way is clear." He didn't actually understand all of those words, but he knew the base commands: *go* and *scout*.

I hissed in pain as Sid launched himself from my shoulder, his sharp talons cutting deep, but the adrenaline coursing through my blood from the discovery insulated me from the worst of the pain. I watched him fly up the hallway, wings flapping silently, and vanish around the corner. If he snapped his beak when he returned to me, then the way wasn't clear.

I followed, steps slowed by the necessity for silence. Sid returned as I neared the corner, and I tilted my head to the side, gritting my teeth to brace myself for the pain his landing would bring.

Once Sid was settled—no snap of his beak—I made my way around the corner, heading for the floor-to-ceiling portrait of a red-haired woman posing regally with a German shepherd. It was supposed to be Dani—*the* Dani, Patron of the Telepaths— but thanks to the memories I'd seen while reading Zoe's book, I now knew the resemblance was weak, the hair not even the right shade of red. The ink sketches within Zoe's journal captured Dani's true likeness much better.

I reached for the side of the gilded frame, finding the trick notch and depressing it. After a quick, furtive glance first up the hallway, then back down the way we had come, I pulled the frame away from the wall and slipped into the hidden passage concealed behind it. Blowing out a breath, I pulled the painting back into place and took a moment to regain my bearings.

So much had happened over the course of the night. So much had changed. I had been suspicious of Mother for a while, but now I had hard evidence that she was involved in something truly vile. I couldn't imagine a single thing she could say to justify what I had seen in the resonance from the case, or worse yet, from the vial. No ends could justify those means.

The tears of pain that lingered on the brims of my eyelids transformed, bittering to tears of sorrow and anger. Of rage.

How could she do this? My own mother. *How?* We weren't close, and she was far from the loving, doting mother figure I so often read about in books, but she had done everything on her part to keep me safe all these years. I was her final surviving daughter of four. In my heart, that protectiveness had counted for something, but maybe I'd been deluding myself, clinging to that quality above all others, blinding myself to her wicked truth.

Sid shifted on my shoulder, the influx of physical pain momentarily drowning out the emotional agony. I had to get back to my room. Whatever else needed to be done, that was first and foremost. I could keep Mother out of my head, but if some of the servants or guards found me sneaking about in the early morning, I would have a hard time explaining myself.

Taking a deep breath, I squared my shoulders and started down the passage hidden between the walls. I wasn't the only one who knew about the passages riddling the castle, but most people avoided them—too many rats and spiderwebs. It wasn't that I enjoyed the creepy crawlies, either, but I did like the secrecy. Especially in a castle where secrets were nearly impossible to keep.

I was making my way along the passage that bordered the entry hall when I heard muffled voices. I paused, eyes narrowing as I slowly backpedaled to the peephole hidden behind a two-way mirror.

A pair of guards were escorting a haggard-looking man through the castle, their oiled black leather armor giving them a sinister appearance. These weren't simple castle guards; these were rangers.

I couldn't tell much about their prisoner's clothing, other than it was coated in layers of drying blood. Despite his gruesome appearance, he didn't seem wounded—no limp or hunch or favored arm. His wrists were bound together behind his back, and he walked between the rangers, his head held high and his countenance giving the impression that he couldn't have cared less about being brought into the castle as a prisoner.

"My old man always said honesty is the best policy," the nearer of the two rangers said. "At least, when dealing with Empaths . . ."

The other ranger, grip tight on the prisoner's arm, nodded

slowly. "I just wish she'd stay out of my head," he griped. "Can't a man get some privacy?"

The nearer ranger scoffed. "Maybe it's time to accept that the wench isn't worth the trouble."

The two rangers exchanged a look, then chortled, amused by some joke I didn't understand.

The farther ranger stopped walking suddenly, jerking the prisoner up short beside him. "What was that?" He stared at the prisoner, his eyes narrowed into a glare.

I frowned, leaning in as close as I could get to the peephole. The prisoner must have mumbled something too low for me to hear.

The nearer ranger stopped as well, turning to look back at his buddy, then shifted his attention to the prisoner. "You got something to say, friend?"

When the prisoner didn't respond—didn't even look at him, the ranger drew his dagger and, without hesitation, stabbed the man in the gut.

I gasped, dropping the electric torch and covering my mouth with my hand. The torch landed on my slipper, then rolled a short way down the passage, though I hardly noticed, glued as I was to the peephole and the shocking scene below.

I knew the imperial guards could be cruel, especially in their handling of criminals and the like, but I had never witnessed that cruelty in action before. Even if such brutality was warranted, it was still hard to watch.

I told myself this man—this prisoner—deserved the punishment. I told myself he was a bad person, that he had done terrible things. I told myself these things because I needed to believe them. It was the only way to keep myself from screaming.

Eyes opened wide in horror, I watched as the ranger yanked the dagger free. The prisoner grunted and folded forward, blood dripping onto the floor at his feet.

But as I watched, the flow of blood slowed, then stopped altogether, and the prisoner straightened. He turned to face the man who had stabbed him, back straight and shoulders squared, no hint of pain or fear—or even hostility—on his grimy face.

I inhaled sharply, my eyes opening even wider. I recognized the prisoner. Not because I had seen him before, at least, not with my own eyes. But in resonance after resonance, I had seen him through Zoe's.

A name escaped from my lips, the ghost of a whisper. "Jake."

2

FIN

"*N*o *more death, not because of me.*"

Jake's words weighed heavily on me as I'd recounted to Autumn what happened in the woods and explained why Jake hadn't returned with me. His words continued to loop through my mind as the families of Timmons, Claire, Dallace, and the others fell into despondency upon seeing their slain loved ones wrapped in linen, all of their lives brutally taken before their time. And Jake's words still haunted me as I sat on top of the waterfall, staring into the cresting dawn beyond the ocean.

The boughs of the redwoods behind me creaked and rustled in the coastal breeze that whirred through the canopy, and with it came the salty scent of morning, and the sweetness of the wild fuchsias that crept up the cliffs.

Beast eyed me from his curled up heap beside me, the tip of his tail flicking in time with the distant waves.

I'd never known any place other than the coast where the twenty-foot falls fell into the Pacific Ocean, and the woods separated two completely different worlds of equal, but strangely different threats. Ferals stalked the woods and mountains. They were the last of a species left behind by the outbreak centuries ago. Their minds were too primal to let them die out now—they clung to life, just like we did, only the years of isolation had turned them nearly rabid.

But beyond the mountains and forest, beyond the tree belt, Corvo City bustled. It was a beacon of law and order and supposed safety, where the pure bloods and the poor—the ones who knew nothing but indenturehood to their "betters"—lived out their lives of naivety. Jake had ensured we never saw such a fate, guiding us, generation after generation, in this life of seclusion. I finally understood why being hidden was so important. I'd seen firsthand what could come to pass for all of us.

When I was little, Jake had been a ghost, foretold to come and go throughout the years, visiting each generation in order to prepare them for what might one day come again. Another end. Another battle. Another time to flee. He'd taught us about our past and the importance of our future. He'd trained us every day he was here for war or resistance, equipping us with the knowledge we would need about the harsh world around us, and what ran through our blood. Or rather, *who* ran through our blood.

I glanced back at the cemetery, past the eight fresh mounds covering my fallen friends to the moss-covered headstones that were weather-worn but far from forgotten.

Rebecca Vaughn - 28 AE - Revolutionary and savior. "Fear not the dark, for with it comes peace."

Tom Cartwright - 39 AE - Survivor and grandfather. May you rest in peace with Mom.

Jason Cartwright - 51 AE - Husband. Father. Brother. Hero.

Dani "Red" Cartwright - 52 AE - D, my soul sister, best friend, and an amazing mother. I miss you every day.

My gaze continued down the row, wishing I'd known all of them, so I could remember my ancestors the way Jake still did—Harper, Sanchez, Chris, Carlos, Peter, Sam . . . But my eyes lingered on the next.

Zoe Cartwright - 59 AE - My beloved. The carved knot above her name matched the one on Dani's. I'd heard stories of the first years, about the world before and after the outbreak, the power-hungry fanatics who thought they were gods, and the eradication of the Re-gens. The originals, my ancestors, had fought all their lives to keep us safe. Because our blood and our Abilities were from the purest, most notable people in our history. In a world built on fear and power, we would always be hunted because of that. I understood that now, more than ever.

We'd spent our lives in hiding because evil always seemed to find us. And for what?

I clenched my hands into fists at my sides. *"No more death, not because of me."*

My best friends were dead, Jake was gone, and the Corvo queen knew where we lived. Her rangers could come back, despite their promise not to, and Jake would've given himself up for nothing. He thought I was reckless and rash, and maybe I was sometimes, but Jake wasn't saving anyone by leaving. If anything, he had taken our greatest weapon away when he'd given himself to them.

Beast's head shot up as I rose and began to pace. "Don't look at me like that," I told him. His ears went back and his tail twitched again. I saw myself through his eyes—a red mane of hair, hard, narrowed eyes, and determined strides, but I ignored him. "You don't understand," I grumbled.

Beast's tail lashed, and he growled at me.

Guilt swelled immediately. "I know," I said. "Sorry." I didn't need to use my animal telepathy to know that Beast felt Jake's absence as much as I did. Jake was the one who'd found him when he was a cub, injured in the woods with a broken leg. Like too many innocents, the Ferals had killed his mother and siblings and had left him to starve. Jake had brought Beast to me, an orphan cougar cub for the orphan boy child in need of a friend, and the three of us had shared a bond ever since.

But being angry was easier than the fear and uncertainty I felt imagining Jake's fate. It was easier than accepting the truth that we might never see him again—that *I* might never see him again.

I continued to pace.

"I knew I'd find you here."

I glanced over my shoulder as Autumn stepped around the gravestones.

A small smile curved her lips, though her face was sullen from all that had transpired in the past twelve hours. "I wanted to make sure you were okay."

I shook my head because I wasn't okay. I was angry with Jake, and with myself. "I let him leave," I told her. Jake hadn't only been a teacher to me since the Ferals killed my parents, he'd been one of the few constants in my life.

I dragged my hand over my face, feeling the exhaustion of the past twenty-four hours behind my eyes and at the base of my neck. "I should've told him to screw off, or that I was going with him. I should've—"

"You wouldn't have said that," she countered.

I stopped mid-step and looked at her. "I could've helped him find a different way instead of just accepting it."

Autumn stepped closer, the breeze playing with the loose strands of her blonde hair, but I turned away. Despite her brave face, her eyes didn't lie, and I didn't want to see the pain or fear in them, no matter how much she tried to hide it.

"The rangers will come back for us," I told her. History had repeated itself too many times for it to be any different.

"Fin . . ." She rested her hand on my shoulder. "Look at me." Autumn's voice was adamant. I could hear the strain in it, and my chest tightened. "Finlay," she snapped.

I forced myself to turn around and peered into her green eyes, the only part of us that was similar. "Do you remember them—Mom and Dad?" I asked, wondering about our parents because they were only a shadow in my memory after all these years.

"I was ten years older than you when they died," she said. "Of course I do."

"Father was a farmer and a predominate Telepath," I said, repeating all I really knew about him.

She nodded. "And Mother's strength was nulling."

"And none of it helped protect them," I ground out.

Autumn's brow furrowed and her lips pursed. "This isn't about them," she said softly, and her hands fell back to her sides.

I began to pace again, more frantically this time. "You're right. It's about Jake, and the fact that I know far more about him than I do about my own parents."

"Fin—"

"*He's* been here all these years, not them."

"Finlay."

"No," I said, ignoring the pain in her eyes. "Listen to me." I had the desperate need to make her understand. "He drinks his tea every morning with the sunrise, before everyone wakes up. He helps Cyrus with his aim and grapples with him to make him feel like he's not just a cripple, but that he has a purpose, just like the rest of us. He goes on hikes and hunting trips all the time because he'd rather be alone than in the company of the villagers, except for me; he takes me with him. And no matter where he goes when he gets in one of his moods, or what he does while he's away, he always comes home to us. I know more about him than I know about my own parents, and now he's gone." I pointed toward the fog rolling in over the sea. "Now he's sitting in a cell somewhere or being experimented on, for all we know."

"I understand that you're upset, Fin, but there was nothing you could've done. Don't kid yourself." Her voice harshened a little. "J would've done exactly what he wanted, regardless of anything you said or did, even if that meant he had to tie you up to do it. He's predictable that way."

"How can you pretend to be so calm about this?" I asked, incredulous. "After all the stories he's told, and after all he's lived through—the guy you love is probably never coming back. You can just accept that?"

Her eyebrows narrowed ever so slightly before she could check herself, and then she peered out at the inky blue sea. "J and I are . . ." I expected her to say that they were only a convenience, which would've been a lie, no matter what she told herself. "Complicated," she continued. "Companionship is different from love, for him at least." She took a step closer, her eyes leveled on me. "Our people take priority over *everything* else to him."

"Yeah? And what if they kill him? He can't protect us if he's dead." I said, voicing the thought that had been haunting me since he sent me back to the village yesterday.

"They won't kill him," she said, more certain than I was. "They clearly need him for something." *Which could be much worse than death.* We both thought it, the gravity of her voice expressed as much, even if she didn't say it out loud.

But despite her reassurances and excuses, it didn't feel right to accept any of it. "After so many years of hiding and running, he can't just give in now."

"It's not your call, Fin. He's gone. The decision's been made, and whatever happens, it's what we have to live with."

I shook my head, unwilling to accept that.

"You don't get a choice in this, Fin."

"Yes, I do," I snapped. "He made his choice, now I'm making mine."

Autumn grabbed my arm, her fingers clenching tightly. "Don't be stupid—"

"I'm not going to be stupid, but I can't sit here and do nothing either. You know I can't, and if you didn't have to set an example for everyone else, you'd be figuring out a way to get him back too."

She straightened her shoulders. "We can't fight against the Corvo army."

"We don't have to fight," I said, realizing this is what Jake had been preparing us for. "But I can get intel. I'm the best tracker we have—Jake made sure of that." My mind began to spin a mile a minute, and my thoughts tumbled from my lips. "I can sneak into the city and figure out where they took him. Maybe I can figure out what they want—I can come back with information so we know what's going on. Maybe then we can at least *try* to come up with a plan. It's better than sitting here doing nothing."

Autumn stared at me, her chest heaving as she realized I wasn't going to change my mind. I imagined she thought of every possible way I could get myself killed, and her features pinched.

After a few heartbeats, she ran her fingers through her hair. "For all that is holy," she muttered and shook her head. "Fine."

Beast leapt to his feet, his anticipation humming through me, amplifying my own.

Autumn took a deep, ragged breath then exhaled an exasperated, slightly hysterical laugh. "You'll go, regardless of anything I say, anyway." When her eyes met mine again, they were hard and earnest. "But you better come home, Finlay, or the gods damn you . . ." She shook her finger at me. "You just better come home."

Beast and I exchanged a determined, victorious look, then I regarded my sister again, offering her a nod of agreement. "We promise."

3

DEL

I sat across from my usual companion, Adasia, at the breakfast table in my sitting room and stared out the window. The morning sunlight glittered off the faint ripples dancing over the surface of the moat below. The hills to the north were covered in whirling white windmills. Two rusted red towers peeked over the hillsides, all that remained of the ancient bridge that once connected the inner city to the wildlands across the bay.

I loved this view, especially at dawn and dusk, when golden light made the castle grounds look somehow ethereal, like the window wasn't a window at all, but a painting of this place from another time. Any other day, I could have lost myself in the view, my soul at peace.

But not today.

Today, it seemed wrong for the morning to be so bright when I felt so glum, as though the sun was mocking me with its smug cheeriness. I couldn't stop thinking about the prisoner. About Jake and all the things I had seen when reading Zoe's hand-written words. What did Mother want with him? Curiosity almost overrode my troubled thoughts about the disturbing resonance I had experienced when cleaning up the broken vial of healing elixir. Almost.

As I stared out the window, a small rowboat glided around Tower Rock, the tiny island near the eastern edge of the moat where the Tower of Solitude, the location of Corvo City's most secure prison cell, stood tall and looming. It was where captives with the most dangerous and volatile Abilities were imprisoned. At least, the ones Mother deemed important enough to keep close and alive . . . for a while.

Three people occupied the boat. Two were castle guards. The other was Jake. The instant I recognized him, the whispers returned in full force.

I closed my eyes, and a low groan hummed in my throat. I had *just* gotten rid of the damnable noise, and now it was back, prodding me into action. Couldn't the whispers at least have given me a single day of reprieve?

"Del?" Adasia said. "Are you all right?"

Down below, on Tower Rock, the knights escorted Jake up the stone stairway to the reinforced steel door barring the tower's entrance.

"Del?" Adasia said again, setting her fork on her plate with a faint clink. "Del?" she repeated with more force.

I tore my attention from the window and looked at Adasia but wasn't really seeing her. My thoughts were on the tiny island across the water—on Jake *now*, and on him two and a half centuries in the past.

I blinked, my brain catching up with the here and now. "I'm sorry," I said, focusing on Adasia. "What did you say?"

Adasia cleared her throat—daintily, like she did all things. Adasia was poised and pretty, delicate and gentle. She was the light to my dark. The bend to my break. The calm to my storm. She had been my companion for as long as I could remember, since we were both young girls, and while I genuinely liked her, I couldn't help but wish for a companion with a little more fire.

But then, Adasia hadn't been chosen as my companion with friendship in mind. She had been chosen for her family and her purity. For her Class. For her Ability.

Adasia was a Gauge, and a powerful one. She could suppress or amplify the Abilities of those around her with merely a thought. If anyone tried to use an Ability to hurt me, they would have to take her out first. Conversely, if I ever needed a little boost in the Empath department, she was there.

"Are you feeling all right, Del?" Adasia asked, her brow furrowing as she studied my face. "You don't seem yourself." She glanced down at my plate. "You've barely touched your honey-cakes, and I don't think you've said more than a few words to me all morning. Perhaps you should lie down?"

I glanced down at my plate. The food lay untouched, the fork limp in my hand. I dropped it and sat back in my chair, squeezing my eyes shut and scrubbing my hands over my face. I was exhausted. I had been too wound-up to sleep when I returned to my room earlier this morning, and the lack of rest was wearing me down. That, and the whispers.

"Sorry, Ada," I said, lowering my hands to my lap and opening my eyes. I flashed her a weak smile. "I didn't mean to ignore you." My attention returned to the window. To the tower across the glittering water. "I think I just need some fresh air."

Adasia sat up straighter, her clear blue eyes lighting up. "A walk, then?" Her expression brightened further, and her lips curved into a hopeful grin. "Or shopping? Shall I call for a pair of guards to escort us to the market district?"

"No!" I blurted, the single word coming out more forcefully than I intended, and my focus snapped back to Adasia.

Her eyes widened in surprise.

I carefully fixed my lips in an apologetic smile. "Sorry, I just —" I took a deep breath. "There's a lot going on right now," I said. "I want to walk around the gardens, get some fresh air, clear my head . . . alone."

Adasia's face fell, and her shoulders slumped. I doubted it was the prospect of losing my sparkling company that dampened her mood; rather, she was already mourning the loss of a chance to spend the day in the market district, browsing the merchant stalls and fancifully dressed storefronts.

My expression softened, and the smile was no longer forced. "But you should go shopping, Ada." I pushed back my chair and stood, heading for the fireplace. I pulled the keyring from the pocket of my dressing gown and fit it into the lock on the small chest forged from Elemental steel that held my personal cache of coins. The iridescent, wavy lines that patterned the top of the chest shimmered in the diffused sunlight streaming in through the windows as I lifted the lid. I fished out a few gold cronins from the stash, then shut and relocked the chest.

"I've seen you eyeing the masks displayed in Lady Lisbet's shop window," I said as I returned to the table, standing beside my chair, but not sitting. "Why don't you meet with Lady Lisbet to design a couple of custom masks—one for each of us for the Bicentennial Ball." I held my hand out over the table, offering the cronins to Adasia. "This should cover the deposit."

Adasia's lips parted, and she eyed the small fortune. She smiled, and hesitantly, she reached out and took the coins. "I would be honored, Del," she said, her gaze rising to meet mine.

The Bicentennial Ball had been on her mind for months. All anyone in the inner city could talk about was how they would celebrate the Corvo dynasty's entry into its third century of glory and prosperity. Only the purest and most noble families would celebrate with Queen Corisande—my mother—at the Bicentennial Ball in the Onyx Ballroom, here in Castle Corvo. Mother claimed it would be the grandest affair the gleaming black walls had ever seen.

Adasia couldn't wait. But I could.

I wished I could stop time. Stop the blood rites that would

determine who I would marry. Stop the seven suitors from the outlying kingdoms from ever arriving at all.

I forced a grin, not wanting Adasia to pick up on my souring mood and prod me to talk through my feelings on the matter. Yet again. We'd discussed my impending engagement and marriage ad nauseam, and I couldn't do it again. Not right now.

Adasia's smile faltered, regardless of my intent. "Are you sure you're all right?"

"Stop worrying, Ada," I said, reclaiming my seat and perching on the edge of my chair. I plucked a strawberry from the plate of honeycakes in front of me and popped it into my mouth, flashing Adasia a closed-mouth smile as I chewed. "I'm fine," I assured her, lifting my mug and taking a sip of lukewarm tea.

Adasia's face displayed her internal struggle. She didn't believe me, but her concern for my wellbeing was at odds with her desire to go mask shopping. And her desire won.

I crossed the bridge connecting Castle Corvo to the mainland. The moat was just large enough to surround Castle Corvo and Tower Rock with a protective barrier of water and to soften the imposing appearance of the castle. It did provide a peaceful, almost idyllic setting, with the tree-lined road surrounding the moat and the orange poppies mixed with other wildflowers providing ground cover around the bases of the trees. Birds chirped and sang, the sun shone, and the air carried the faintest hint of the briny sea.

It was an effort to keep my pace slow and steady. I greeted a pair of nobles chatting near the middle of the bridge with a wooden smile, then stepped off the bridge and turned right, starting up the road toward the boathouse. Unless I wanted to swim across the moat to the Tower of Solitude, I would need to borrow a rowboat.

At the sound of a familiar caw, I glanced over my shoulder and spotted Sid gliding toward me. He usually warned me of his approach so I could prepare for his landing.

I raised my arm as the raven swooped down, flapping his wings at the last minute to slow his descent. His talons gripped the leather bracer covering my forearm. He took a moment to regain his balance before hopping up the ribbed leather strip lining the upper portion of my sleeve and reclaiming his usual perch on my shoulder. The tips of his feathers tickled my neck as he settled in.

"Good morning, Sid," I said, tilting my head away from him so I could see him better. A smear of something wet glistened on his obsidian beak. Blood, no doubt. "You look like you've been up to no good," I murmured.

Sid ignored me, twisting his neck to preen the feathers under his wing.

"Well, I hope you had a good breakfast," I told him, returning my attention to the way ahead. "We have work to do..."

When we reached the boathouse, I sent Sid off on a mission to distract the boat master while I shielded my mind and snuck down to the dock and borrowed one of the smaller rowboats. Oars in hand, I quickly rowed the boat around to the far side of Tower Rock, the whispers seeming to grow louder with each and every stroke. I guided the boat into a small alcove hidden between the sheltering roots of a cypress tree and tucked the oars safely inside the boat as I waited for Sid to join me.

A few minutes later, Sid landed on a branch overhead. I tied off the boat and awkwardly climbed onto the sloping shore of the small island, leaning on the trunk of the cypress for balance. I peered up the short but steep, rocky incline to the tower jutting into the sky. Getting up there wouldn't be easy. Getting into the tower unnoticed would be even harder.

Blowing out a breath, I started to climb.

"Uh oh!" Sid croaked as I clambered over the ledge bordering the base of the tower. He leapt off the branch with a caw.

I froze and looked up.

Sid circled overhead, above the imposing figure of a knight, silhouetted by the blinding sunlight. He stood a few paces away, hands on his hips, his expression hidden in shadow.

I had been noticed, which left me with a single option. An option which, if discovered, would mean death for me. But I had no choice. The whispers drove me onward. I had to find out why Jake was here—why now, right after I found Zoe's book—and what his connection was to the whispers. My sanity depended on it.

I raised a hand to block out the sun and finally got a good look at the knight's face. Tanned skin and amber eyes. Strong, angular features. Just the faintest hint of stubble on his jawline. A lump of icy dread settled in my belly.

"You shouldn't be here, princess," the knight said.

I stood up, taking a moment to brush my hands off before straightening. "Good morning to you, too, Garath," I said, giving the strapping young knight a once-over. "What are *you* doing here?" I snorted a laugh. My banter was all bravado. Inside, I was panicking. "What did you do—pluck the wrong flower?"

Garath had a certain reputation with the ladies of the noble houses. And with the ladies of the less noble houses. He was usually stationed in the throne room, serving Mother. Guarding a prisoner was a clear demotion.

Regardless, it was no wonder that he had discovered my attempt to sneak into the tower. He was a Telepath, and a powerful one, not limited to humans or small geographic regions like so many of our generation. Even with my mental guard up, he'd likely spotted me through the eyes of his animal familiars and had been tracking me since I'd left the boathouse.

I hated what I was about to do. Beyond the fact that using the more dangerous facet of my Ability exhausted me, Garath was one of the few of Mother's knights that I genuinely liked. He wasn't in it for the power, but for the good of the kingdom. At twenty-two, he was only a few years older than me, and he had often been my sparring partner during my combat training sessions over the years. This world wasn't a safe place, especially not for those in power. There was a reason I was Mother's sole heir . . .

Of course, since Garath had helped train me, that meant he knew most of my tricks. He wasn't about to let me simply reach out and touch him. I would have to improvise.

"Why are you here, princess?" Garath asked.

"I thought we were past all that 'princess' stuff," I said, raising my eyebrows as I took a step toward him.

Garath stepped backward, keeping pace with me. His armor was hardened black leather reinforced with carbon fiber chain mail. I would need a clear patch of skin for my forbidden trick to work, but Garath was covered from boots to mid-neck. That left his face. Awkward, to say the least.

I took another step toward him, but this time, I purposely caught the toe of my boot on the sharp edge of exposed rock and tumbled forward. Into Garath's open arms.

As he helped me regain my footing, I tilted my head back, my eyes meeting his, and reached up, cupping the side of his face with my hand.

Garath's amber eyes widened, and his expression softened. "Del...," he breathed, his gaze searching mine.

"I'm sorry," I whispered, just a moment before I brushed my lips against his. And pushed my way into his mind.

Within Garath's memories, I found the moment before he noticed my mental signature in the boathouse and stretched that moment out, blanketing it over all that had happened between then and now. But I didn't stop there. I spliced in a simple illusion, making Garath believe he had scouted around to the side of the tower in search of a mysterious but benign noise. I clipped myself and Sid from his perception, making us relatively invisible for the time being—so long as we didn't make any big movements or loud noises, he wouldn't notice we were there. I changed his memories, manipulated his mind. Some might call it mind control. It was an exhausting trick, and extremely dangerous.

The eradication of all Controllers was the base upon which the Corvo kingdom had been founded. Every day, I struggled with the possibility that I was one of them. I could make people change their minds. I could make them believe something other than the truth. By altering their perception—their memories—I could control them.

Garath's focus grew distant, almost like he was looking through me, and he let go. He looked around, then frowned and turned his back to me.

As he made his way back to the tower entrance, I fished the pendant watch out from my collar and set the timer for eight minutes. The altered perception effect should hold a minute or two longer than that, but it would begin to degrade shortly after. If I wanted to get away unnoticed and ensure he had no memory of me being here, I would have to leave Tower Rock by then. I could always tamper with his mind again, but each successive touch to the same memory patch would decrease the stability of the patch.

Blowing out a breath, I followed Garath to the front of the tower. I slyly plucked the keyring from his belt and used the largest, most complex key to unlock the heavy steel door. As quietly as I could, I opened the door, then turned back to Garath and carefully returned the keyring to his belt.

My gaze drifted up to his familiar features. If I had any kind of choice in the matter, I thought I could grow to love Garath, given the chance. In another time, another place, we could have been happy together, but the choice of whom to love wasn't given to princesses of this kingdom.

"I'm so sorry," I repeated, the words barely audible. And then I turned away from him and slipped into the tower, waiting for Sid to swoop in before easing the door shut behind me.

The whispers were even louder inside the tower, seeming to echo off the lead-lined cement walls. As my limited time continued to tick by, I rushed up the spiraling staircase, only slowing when the landing at the top came into view. Sid clung to my shoulder, his talons nearly piercing through the leather lining. A couple more steps and I could see the first few iron bars of the square prison cell built into the chamber at the top of the tower, then the foot of a bed in the center of the cell. And then, finally, I could see the man I had come here for.

Jake sat on the edge of the thin mattress, his bare feet on the floor and his elbows on his knees, his head hanging as he stared at the polished cement floor. He wore a simple tunic and trousers of fine-woven cotton, dyed bright red to make him conspicuous should he try to flee. His clean skin made it obvious that he'd been allowed to bathe before being sent to his solitary prison.

I stepped on the landing and approached the bars. The whispers were suddenly quiet, and I couldn't tell if the faint hum that filled their absence was all in my head or caused by the electric current charging the cell bars.

I took one final step toward the bars, then stopped and cleared my throat.

Jake raised his head and looked at me, his focus shifting from my face to the raven on my shoulder and back. He narrowed his eyes, his stare scrutinizing. With a derisive laugh, he looked away, focusing on the wall through the electrified bars.

I stood there, unsure of what to say. I hadn't actually thought this far ahead. I had met a few Healers, but Jake was by far the oldest—by a century or two. How was I supposed to talk to someone like him? To a Patron?

"Did your mother send you?" Jake asked, his voice a low rumble.

My eyes widened, and my heartbeat sped up. I suddenly felt too hot and kind of sweaty all over, as nerves sent a subtle tremor throughout my body. "No," I said, swallowing reflexively. "She doesn't know I'm here. No one does." I cleared my throat again. "I came to talk to you, but I don't have much time. I saw the rangers bring you in, and—" I licked my lips, shooting a quick glance over my shoulder. "I know who you are."

Jake's attention returned to me, a hint of curiosity in his stare. "And who exactly do you think I am?"

I took a tiny step closer to the deadly cell bars. "You're Jake," I said. "The Patron. The Healer."

Jake laughed under his breath, but there was no humor in the sound. He stood and casually approached, his eyes locking with mine. As he drew precariously close to his electrified cage, I fought the urge to take a step backward.

"What do you want, princess?" Jake asked, leaning ever closer to the bars.

On my shoulder, Sid ruffled his feathers, snapping his beak in warning. Again, I glanced behind me, making sure we were still alone.

"Because it's obvious you're not supposed to be here," he added.

"I want to understand," I told him, meeting his stare. "Where have you been all this time? And why are you here—now?"

Jake leaned back a little and crossed his arms over his chest, his eyes narrowing once more. "You're an Empath, aren't you? Can't you dig through my mind to find what you need?"

I shook my head, hesitating for a moment. "I'm not that kind of Empath," I finally admitted. "I have to be touching someone to see or feel anything."

Jake frowned and grunted. "If your Ability is so limited, then how did you get in here?" he asked.

I averted my gaze to the floor, my cheeks heating. I could feel Jake's weighty stare.

"How about a trade," he said. "A question for a question. An answer for an answer."

My eyes returned to his, but only for a moment.

His head tilted slightly. "A truth for a truth."

I swallowed roughly, weighing my options. I came here for a reason. To get some answers. Was I really about to let a little thing like fear get in my way?

My stare locked on the floor, I nodded.

"Then tell me," Jake said, "how did you get in here?"

I sighed. "I tricked Garath—the knight guarding the tower," I explained. I hesitated before damning myself completely, then barreled onward. "I created an illusion—in his mind. He won't remember that he saw me here, so long as I leave before the illusion fades."

I had never told anyone about that facet of my Ability. Not even Mother. Especially not Mother. If she found out, there was a good chance she would have me killed.

In my peripheral vision, I watched Jake study me. The seconds ticked by, precious time slipping away as I awaited his judgment. Would he see me the same way Mother would, if she ever found out, especially after the horrors Controllers had committed during Jake's time? Or worse, would Mother dig it out of his mind? Would she even need to? Would he volunteer the information?

"Some might call that mind control," Jake finally said, voicing my greatest fear.

My heart hammered in my chest, and I felt slightly lightheaded.

"But not me," Jake said. "Tom was the same," he added. "Zoe could do it a bit, too."

I dragged my stare up to Jake's face. To his eyes. What was he saying? What was he telling me—that two of the beloved originals, Zoe and her father, were like me?

Another of those derisive laughs rumbled in Jake's chest. "Your fear is understandable," he said. "You've never known a true Controller since there aren't any left. All you have are stories and lore to compare yourselves to now, but I can tell you this—you're no Controller."

"I don't think my mother will see it the same way," I said, my voice hushed and frail.

"Who says she'll ever find out?" he said, his brow lifting wryly. While I appreciated the sentiment, it was a lie. We both knew it. Mother was a renowned Empath, known across all the kingdom for being able to dig the deepest, darkest secrets out of her enemies' minds.

Mother would be able to pluck the information from Jake with minimal effort. Unless I created an illusion, overwriting his memory of my visit. She would be able to detect my tampering eventually if she looked hard enough, but at least it would buy me some time. *And* if Jake was no longer her prisoner, then she wouldn't have access to his mind. I would have no choice—free him, or kill him.

I couldn't help but suspect I had just stepped into a carefully laid trap.

The corner of Jake's mouth lifted, his lips displaying the hint of a smile. "Do what you have to do," he said. "But before you wipe my memory, I promised you answers to your questions."

I blinked, surprised by the sudden subject change.

"I've been in hiding," Jake started, "with my family. And I'm here because your mother threatened to kill them—to kill more innocents than she already has—if I didn't turn myself in." After a brief pause, he added, "And no, I don't know why she wants me, though I have a few guesses. Regardless of why, the slaughter of my people needed to end."

I had no words. I simply stared at Jake, my lips parted and my eyes opened wide, horrified by his claim. "I—I'm so sorry," I said. "I had no idea she was—" I shook my head, my mind reeling.

Was I really surprised? Mother was ruthless. She was brilliant and strong and determined. But was she a murderer? My stomach knotted as I recalled the resonance from the broken vial in the vault. The man writhing in pain as his blood was drained from his body.

Yes, Mother was definitely capable of murder.

I straightened, squaring my shoulders, and moved a little closer to the bars. "I want to help you—you and your people," I told him. "What can I do?"

Jake's jaw twitched as he stared at me, and a strange mixture of relief and curiosity lit his eyes, as if he was trying to figure me out. "You really want to help?"

I nodded hurriedly.

"Find out what the queen wants with me," he said. "What's she after that's worth the deaths of so many?"

A chiming filled the chamber, and I glanced down at the pendant watch resting against my chest.

Sid ruffled his wings. "Time's up!"

4

FIN

The waters were choppy and sloshed into the hull of my boat as I tied it to the top of a sunken sailboat mast protruding from the dark waters beneath the cliff's edge. My fishing boat wasn't the best our village had built, and though the cedar planks were seven years weatherworn, it was still strong and reliable.

With no bridge connecting the wild headlands to the lands belonging to the Corvo kingdom, crossing the bay by boat had been my most direct option. Fishing in calm waters on a sunny day with Claire and Dallace bickering on the bow was one thing, but the turbulent uppercuts of the white caps were another, and I was glad to be so close to dry land.

My heart ached at the thought of my dead friends, but I pushed the pain aside and tightened the rope around the rusted mast.

Heaving a steadying breath, I peered up at the sandstone cliffs. The towering cypress trees bent to the will of the wind, and it would be a harried climb to the top, to say the least, but this spot would have to do. Here, where the boat was hidden on the outskirts of the forest, was the safest place to come and go undetected near Corvo City.

Beast leapt onto the dry cliff, unable to leave the sloshing boat fast enough, and settled at the roots of one of the trees growing out from the side of the mountain. With his ears lowered and his coat wet with saltwater, he glowered at me and began to lick himself clean.

"It's not my fault you're wet," I told him. "Blame the royals—hell, blame Jake, if you want, but don't blame me."

The boat rocked as I donned my fox fur cape and shrugged on my pack. Then, I slung my bow and quiver over my shoulder. With a final gust of wind and a splash of the waves over my already drenched clothes, I gripped onto the rocky cliffside, found purchase for my foot, and pulled myself up. My boots slipped on a sandy crevasse, but having always been a good climber, I found my footing easily and gripped the sandstones harder and began to climb.

The late afternoon sun pressed against my back, and I figured that once it set, I would be grateful for the furs to keep me warm, even if I felt ridiculous wearing them. Though I'd never been to Corvo City, I knew they traded with outsiders for goods and wares all the time. A fur trader seemed a safe enough bet to get me into the city, but it was what would happen once I was inside that I still needed to iron out. Knowing Beast would have to remain outside the city walls to avoid being captured or killed didn't ease my anxieties either.

The rocks made for decent grips and stepping-stones, and I quickly passed Beast up the side of the cliff as he licked the salt from his coat.

"There's no time for that," I told him, earning a thwarted growl in return. "You can primp and preen later." My shoulders and neck strained as I continued to the top, and Beast growled at me again before he leapt past, looking smugly down at me. *I'd race you, but we already know I'd win.*

"Bastard," I muttered and continued to climb.

The waves crashed against the rocks below, and while heights had never bothered me much, sand in my mouth always did. I scowled up at Beast as he jumped from one perch to another, raining dust and gravel down on me.

After an entire day of rowing in rough waters, my forearms and biceps ached with fatigue, but I pushed past it. I had to stay focused. I had to ignore the wind whipping by me, sending a wash of chills over my dampened skin. And with one last heave, I made the final climb to the top.

As I pulled myself over the edge of the cliff and onto flatter ground, I gave an exhale of relief, for my muscles' sake, and peered across the bay into the fog-shrouded wildland. Home felt like an entire world away, and I fleetingly hoped this wasn't the last time I would ever see it. My chest tightened at the thought, but I pushed the possibility away. I had more immediate concerns.

I'd expected there would be city guards patrolling the land surrounding Corvo City, whether it was a telepathic survey or a forest search party to ensure there was no incoming danger. Either way, I was prepared. The minds I could sense, near and far, were blocked as I focused on them, closing my mind to theirs and nulling their Abilities against me as I hid my mind signature from any Telepaths who would be able to sense me as well. The more intently I focused, the more the tingling mind signatures in the periphery of my consciousness dulled, quickly turning to nothing.

Nulling was the only sure way for me to go unnoticed by prodding minds, and getting through the inner walls of the city was paramount if I was going to find Jake, or glean any information worth knowing while I was in there. And while the guise of a fur trader seemed like a solid plan to get into the city, approaching from the opposite side of the peninsula, away from the shipping port, might alarm them, which meant I needed to remain invisible and unthreatening for as long as possible.

Sitting a few feet in front of me, Beast growled, goading *me* to hurry up this time. He flicked his tail, impatiently waiting for our adventure to start. Nothing about Beast was patient, which was why we got along so well. But he was right. The longer I waited, the worse off Jake might be, and I didn't want to think about what sort of damage the queen and her people could have done to him in the span of the past twenty-four hours.

I glanced up at the sun as it began its descent to the horizon, then turned and followed Beast into the protective cover of the cypress forest. We still had five or six miles to go before we reached the city, and I needed to formulate the rest of my plan.

We hadn't been walking more than twenty minutes when the path became less sandy and my boots fell on asphalt. I paused, then stared down at my feet. *A road.* Not like a deer trail or path carved out in the foliage, but a hard, manmade road that was barely visible through a layer of dirt. I'd only ever seen a real, ancient road once before, when Jake took me and a few others on a two-week trek north of home, toward one of the abandoned communities on the other side of the mountains.

Beast brushed through the juniper as we continued deeper into the woods, following the road east, toward the city. I tried to imagine what this forgotten world had looked like three hundred years ago and where, exactly, the road I was following was taking me.

After another thirty minutes, Beast caught wind of a mule deer and veered right, heading into the trees to chase down his dinner. My own stomach rumbled as I realized how long it had been since Autumn made me eat a goopy bowl of porridge before casting off. Wasting no time, I pulled a biscuit and a piece of jerky from my pack, took a few gulps of water from my deerskin, and continued on my way. I needed the fuel to keep going, and I had a long night ahead of me; I didn't think a break was coming anytime soon.

I bit into the biscuit and immediately spit it into the dirt, brushing the excessively salty crumbs from my lips. Autumn was the best sister I had—the *only* sister I had—and I loved her more than anyone, but she couldn't cook to save her life. That was Jake's thing and sometimes mine. I tossed the biscuit into the bushes for some poor, unsuspecting animal to find later and tore a piece of venison off between my teeth.

I'd only made it a few more yards before I stopped. A cemetery of buildings stretched out before me, the old parts of the city that were long forgotten. Crumbled facades were half-buried in the sandpits that had swallowed up so much of the peninsula centuries ago. It was why Corvo City was so well poised on the highest part of the cliffs, atop a foundation of unshakable sandstone, surrounded by sandpits and a maze of ruins. It would've been difficult to find my way to Corvo City through the forest if I hadn't had some knowledge of it, thanks to Jake, and Beast's keen sense of smell. I'd studied Corvo City's location and listened with awe as Jake recounted the creation of it centuries ago.

Long before Corvo City, Herodson's mind-controlling followers had taken up his cause, even after his death, and forced thousands of unwitting people into slavery. They established the new world exactly as they wanted it, with new settlements and laws upheld with deadly force.

But everything changed after the Great Awakening in 30 AE, when survivors finally broke away, and builders amassed on the peninsula to construct a safe haven for the free people of the New Republic. Survivors with Abilities came from all around the continent with the hope of protection and a naïve wish for a shared sense of community. Little did they know the Corvo elitists who had stepped in with their powerful Abilities wouldn't only help the freed people to build a safe haven, but they would build a kingdom through which the Corvo dynasty would rule, as power-hungry as any survivor before them.

The closer I drew to the ruined city of San Francisco, the more unnerved I became. The faded photographs I'd seen of the ancient city were nothing compared to the decaying buildings I saw through the trees. Some of the structures had collapsed, while others stood ominously, as if not even the wind could knock them down. It was an eerie playground of rust and ruin, but I couldn't avoid it, so I continued through.

People had lived here once, and even if I knew their bodies were long gone, I could imagine the graveyard of the dead a few layers beneath my feet.

Cypress boughs creaked in the breeze, and dust whipped through the abandoned city, making it howl in protest as I trudged through the sand dunes formed along the streets. Buildings were toppled with cracks and gaping holes. Illegible, eroded metal signs were covered in grapevines. Rotted wooden poles jutted sporadically from the sand, leaning a dozen feet out of the ground with frayed wires snapping in the breeze.

Corvo City was close, I just needed to see how close and make sure I was heading in the right direction. I looked for the highest vantage point in a sea of ruin and walked over to a metal shell of what appeared to be an old automobile of some sort— long and boxy—that angled a couple of dozen feet toward the sky. I climbed up, gripping the corroded metal for purchase as it heaved a tinny groan with each of my steps.

Determined not to fall and break my neck, I balanced myself as I reached the top, then straightened and peered out into the gray evening sky. The crumbled city stretched on, caked in rust and weathered by time. Nature, however, had run its course too, softening the harshness of what wasn't buried with overgrown bramble bushes and ivy.

I squinted as the last rays of the sun glinted off something metallic in the distance. Then I realized what it was, part of Corvo City—a bell in a tower, perhaps, or a monument, which stood sentry over the city from atop its hill. Lush green fanned out around the castle, met by a wall that shimmered in the dying light; a labyrinth of buildings and streets snaked their way down the hillside, disappearing behind another wall that stood between me and Jake.

It's a fortress, I realized. Walls upon walls separated the royal family from the rest, and I feared getting through the city gates would be the least of my problems. Running my hands over my face, I sighed, pushing away the exhaustion of the day. I was a couple of miles out still, but if I was quick, I could get to the city by the time full night set in.

I'll know Jake's fate soon enough. Gulping down my fear, I slid off the side of my rusted lookout perch. Jake didn't know it, but he was counting on me to save him. Autumn was counting on me too, and no matter how many walls and guards stood between us, I was resolved: I *would* find Jake.

My boots had barely hit the ground when I felt another wave of unease, but it wasn't mine this time. I knew instantly it came from Beast, and I opened my mind to his even more. Panic hit me like a gale of wind, and I ran in his direction. He was near, in a thick-barred cage that flashed in my mind's eye, and he was scared for his life.

My legs carried me faster as I used his mind signature to find him. *I'm coming!* I told him, but I could feel his fear as if it were my own. Clawing, heart-hammering, perilous fear. He growled and yowled in the distance. *I'm coming! Hold on!*

I saw the Ferals through Beast's eyes before I rounded the corner of a crumbled cement heap, my feet halting even if I wanted to run straight for him. I lingered in the shadows of dying sunlight, out of sight, as two Ferals lifted their spears and stalked toward him.

I lifted my bow and pulled an arrow from my quiver. I would

have to be quick to get them both. As I took aim, I realized they weren't like the other Ferals I'd come across before. There were only two of them, not a family or a looting gang or hunting party. It appeared to be a mother and her daughter with wild, unkempt hair and dirt on their faces. Their clothes were torn to almost nothing, as if the things they wore were all they had.

I drew the bowstring back, prepared to let it loose as they began poking the points of their spears through the cage bars at Beast, but my fingers tightened on the string, and I hesitated. They weren't evil-looking creatures, but pathetic and wretched. *They're starving*, I realized.

The mother had broad, bony shoulders, and she rammed her spear through the wooden bars again with emaciated arms, barely missing Beast as he cowered deeper into the corner of the cage. The woman uttered indiscernible words, and the girl beside her shrieked something back in reply.

They jabbed their spears harder, and Beast lashed out at them. He hissed and growled and clawed at the cage as they tried to poke him again, knocking the girl's spear out of her hands this time. I cursed myself for hesitating. They were going to kill him.

Suddenly, they spun around, lifting their noses to the air with wide fearful eyes, and an idea dawned on me. I wasn't sure if they could smell me or if they could sense something else, but whatever it was, they were afraid. *Of the rangers?*

I knew Ferals had been hunted down and killed off to protect the city, just as the queen's soldiers had tried to do to us. And like us, the Ferals didn't stand a chance against an army of Ability-wielding rangers, and the Ferals' fear of the rangers was an advantage to me.

Flexing my consciousness, I grabbed hold of their mind signatures and used the only non-fatal weapon in my arsenal, even if it was one that would take its toll on me. Telepathically, I showed them what I'd seen yesterday, praying they feared the rangers as much as they should. I showed them the dozen men holding their guns point-blank at my hunting party as they circled us, shouting and shooting without an ounce of hesitation.

I watched the Feral mother's eyes widen, and she grunted. She muttered incoherent words louder and more urgently this time as she crouched down, searching the dilapidated streets around her frantically for movement as she tried to discern what was happening. I projected every image and fear. More grunts. More shrieks as the Ferals peered around, frantically scanning the desolate streets.

The mother's brow pinched, but as she turned back for the cage, pushing her uncertainty aside in need of food, I realized simply seeing the rangers and the havoc they caused wasn't enough to sway her away from her evening meal.

I thought harder and pried deeper into her mind. The pain I felt exuding so much effort was overwhelming, but the woman needed to see it. All of it. I let the painful memories pour into both of their minds as I replayed my memory of my friends falling to the ground one by one, all while I begged the man with fire shooting from his palms into my best friends' chests to stop. I felt the rage and helplessness, and my body shook with fear and desperation.

My mind continued to throb, and sweat beaded on my brow, but I blared my memories until they were booming and the forms of the cowering women were blurred by tears.

I gathered a handful of rocks behind me and tossed them in the opposite direction. The sound of them ricocheted off metal signs and poles, echoing in the air.

That was all it took to send the mother and daughter sprinting away with shrieks of fear as they fleetingly looked back at Beast. They would go hungry, but at least they weren't dead. I wasn't sure I could bear having that on my conscience.

When they were out of sight, I ran to Beast's cage a few yards away. He chirped with relief and licked at my hand as I gripped the wooden bar for leverage, pounding the latch open with the bone hilt of the knife I pulled from my belt.

When the latch broke, Beast barreled out before I could open it all the way, and together, we ran back into the cover of the forest.

Only when the Ferals' mind signatures were far away, did I allow myself to stop and breathe. Fleetingly, I regretted using that facet of my Ability, knowing the recovery time it would cost me when I had little time to waste. But killing them hadn't felt like an option, either.

Head still pounding, I fell to my knees under a canopy of cypress. Beast nudged me, purring in relief, and I rested my head against his and tried to catch my breath. My chest heaved, and adrenaline pumped through my veins.

If the next twenty-four hours were going to be anything like the last, I needed to rest. I rocked back on my heels, Ability-overload and exhaustion settling over me like a weighted blanket. My limbs were suddenly too heavy, and my mind was a foggy mess.

Rising to my feet, I ran my hands over my face. "Holy hell," I rasped.

Beast looked at me with an "it took you long enough to help me" expression, and guilt washed over me.

"Yeah, yeah." I leaned over and playfully pushed his annoying face away from me, grateful I hadn't had to resort to the bow. "Don't start with me. I need a minute." Suddenly desperate for sleep, I nodded to a bed of ivy growing around the trees.

Shakily, I walked past Beast, ignoring his playful swat at my legs as I made my way to my temporary bed. I dropped my pack and bow by the trunk of the tree and plopped down beside it, wrapping my fur cape tighter around me. "We'll sleep, just for a little while," I told him.

With a languid stretch, Beast walked over and curled up into a purring heap beside me. Before another minute could pass, sleep consumed me.

5

DEL

I dodged the fist flying toward my face but didn't notice the hand reaching for my forearm or the foot hooking around the back of my ankle. Before I knew what was happening, my back slammed against the floor, closely followed by my head, and the air whooshed from my lungs. For a heart-stopping moment, I couldn't catch my breath, and time slowed to a crawl; the world around me bleeding of all sights and sounds.

"You really want to help?"

I blinked, Jake's weary face swimming in and out of my mind's eye.

"Find out what the queen wants with me. What's she after that's worth the deaths of so many?"

I blinked again, and my sense of the here and now flooded back as I sucked in a breath. The blood rushing through my veins was a roar in my ears, and the soft light of the electric torches set into the walls of the training room suddenly seemed too bright. I squinted, bringing the face staring down at me into focus.

Garath's strong features were drawn, his amber eyes alight with concern. A second face joined his. Hills, my training instructor, looked far from impressed and not the least bit worried. Her hawkish stare was as scrutinizing as ever.

"Where's your head, girl?" she said, her eyes narrowing. "That's the fifth time tonight you've let Garath take you down." She sniffed. "It's not like you."

Hills was a middle-aged ex-ranger, taken off duty eight years ago, on my tenth birthday, with the sole purpose of taking charge of my hand-to-hand combat training. Her gruff manner disguised a tender heart, and she was like a second mother to me. In many ways, she was a vast improvement over my actual mother.

With a heavy exhale, I sat up. Garath offered me a hand to stand, and I accepted it, however reluctantly. He should have been afraid to touch me. He would have been, had he known what I had done.

"Thanks," I said, avoiding meeting his eyes. I felt terrible for what I had done to him this morning. I had betrayed him in the worst possible way—by messing with his head. And he didn't even know it.

Staring at a random spot on the padded floor mat, I rubbed the place where my neck met my right shoulder. That last fall must have tweaked a muscle because I could already feel a crick forming in my neck.

Hills stepped in front of me, standing closer than was comfortable, and peered up at me. "Think you can get your head on straight, or should we call it a night?" she asked, tone softer than her words warranted. "The last thing I need is a tongue lashing from the queen for letting Garath play too rough with you before the Bicentennial Celebration."

I looked her in the eye, letting her see how unamused I was by her mention of the looming festivities. But something behind Hills caught my eye, gleaming gold on the wall of the training room. The enormous antique map of what had once been called the "Bay Area". It was solid gold, created by a second-century

Elemental artist who specialized in the manipulation of precious metals into replicas of maps of the world *before*. The moment my focus shifted to the map, the whispers started up again, faint but insistent.

They wanted something. Again. The whispers always wanted something, and I now knew from experience that the only way to make them stop was to give them what they wanted. And right now, I would have bet my life they wanted me to get a closer look at the map.

"Well, girl?" Hills said. "What's it going to be?"

Ignoring Hills, I brushed past her, heading for the map. The whispers grew louder as I approached, drawing me in. I scanned different parts of it as I moved closer. The major cities were labeled—Oakland, San Jose, and the old name for Corvo City, San Francisco. My eyes moved over the smaller cities and towns. The coastlines. The Bay.

By the time I stopped in front of the map, the whispers were a roar in my ears. Until my stare landed on a tiny island north of San Francisco.

Alcatraz.

The whispers stopped, the gong of my heartbeat filling the sudden silence. Three centuries ago, Alcatraz was a prison on an isolated island. It still was—only now called Prison Island, one of the few places from *before* that retained its purpose.

What did it mean? What were the whispers trying to tell me?

"Del?" Garath said from right behind me.

I started, one hand clutching my chest, directly over my racing heart, and spun around to face him.

Garath took a step back, hands raised in placation. That concern from moments ago was still etched across his face. "Are you all right?"

I furrowed my brow, wishing he would stop being so nice to me. I didn't deserve it. I shook my head, laughing under my breath, then glanced over my shoulder at the map. At the gleaming, golden lump that made up Prison Island. "No," I said, more to myself than to him. "I don't think I am all right."

Realizing how strange I must have sounded to him, I tore my eyes from the map and looked at Garath, flashing him a weak smile. "I think I hit my head a little too hard on that last drop." I rubbed the back of my neck. "I'll be fine," I added. "I just need to rest. I've had a lot on my mind."

"Yeah," Garath said, the corners of his mouth angling downward. "The Bicentennial is only ten days away . . ."

My expression soured. "I thought we made a deal," I said, a sharp edge to my voice. He wasn't really talking about the Bicentennial Celebration, but the coinciding blood rites competition, which would result in the selection of my future consort. Mother had thought it a grand idea to lump the two events together, now that I was eighteen and officially of age. Me, not so much. "*You* wouldn't bring *that* up anymore," I reminded Garath, "and *I* wouldn't tell the noble ladies about your little misunderstanding at the Countess—"

Garath's eyes widened, and he coughed suddenly, turning away from me and facing Hills. "Well," he said in a rush, "you heard the princess, Hills. We're done for the night." He retreated to the corner where he had stashed his training bag.

I chuckled as I watched him, but when Hills stepped into my line of sight, her arms crossed over her chest, and the spark of humor within me faded.

"I know this isn't an easy time for you, Del," Hills said, "but your training is more important now than ever before." She uncrossed her arms and moved closer, stopping to stand just out of arm's reach. "You will be welcoming a relative stranger into your personal space." Personal *space*, she had said, not personal *life*. Hills knew me well enough to know *that* wasn't an option. "Once the suitors arrive, you must always be on your guard. And once the blood rites are over and your consort is chosen, you must treat him as you would a foe in battle. Never turn your back to him. Never trust him." Her voice was filled with fervor, her eyes with conviction. "And never—*never*—let him into your heart, for then he will own you, and through you, he will own the kingdom."

I gulped, and then I nodded.

"Best to give your heart to another *before* the blood rites," Hills said, glancing over her shoulder at Garath, who was in the corner, chugging from a waterskin. "Then it will be safe from the greedy hands of your soon-to-be consort."

I stared at Garath, my neck and cheeks heating. "What are you saying?" I asked, my voice a little hoarse. I cleared my throat, forcing my focus back to Hills.

Hills stepped closer, her features softening as she rested a hand on my shoulder. Flashes of a younger version of her played through my mind, memories of her time as a guard before she became a ranger. Memories of a woman. Memories that made my blush deepen and my heart break.

Hills squeezed my shoulder. "I'm saying be with him. Give your heart a gift—something for it to hold on to." Her stare hardened. "And then lock your heart away and throw out the key."

My eyes stung as I processed her words. I had never—not ever—considered breaking my chastity vow. Of course, I had fantasized about being with another, with someone of my choosing. Oh, who was I kidding? I had fantasized about being with Garath. But I'd never actually entertained the possibility of going through with it. The fantasy was a fruit made sweeter by its impossibility.

But then I thought about the chastity vow. About the purpose for it—to ensure that my heir was as strong as possible. As *pure* as possible. All the suitors were Empaths, meaning my heir would be an Empath as well, just as every Corvo queen had been for the last two centuries. Always a woman to guarantee the continuation of the bloodline, and always an Empath to ensure strength of leadership and an undeceivable nature.

The vow said nothing about purity of heart; all that mattered was purity of body. Even someone as inexperienced as me knew there were many ways to share the physical expression of love.

"I—" The words caught in my throat, and I coughed to clear it. "I shall think on your advice." I covered Hills's hand with my own. "Thank you, Hills, truly." I squeezed her hand, then released it.

"We'll take the day off tomorrow," Hills said. "Rest up."

Eyes on the floor and thoughts spinning, I crossed the room and slipped out into the hallway, heading for the corridor that would carry me back to the royal living quarters. After my conversation this morning with Jake, and now this, I was in desperate need of some time alone to think. And rest. My mind felt fuzzy from the lack of sleep, and I doubted I would be able to think clearly until I could shut my eyes, just for a little while.

"Hey! princess!" Garath called out, his boots slapping the stone floor of the hallway behind me as he jogged to catch up. "Del," he amended before I could correct him. "I'm heading down to the kitchens for a snack." He fell in step beside me. "Care to join me?"

Out of the corner of my eye, I watched his lips twist with a wry smile.

"I bet we could sneak a bottle of nightwine from the cellar . . ."

I slowed, stopping in the convergence between two corridors Garath stopped as well, turning to face me. The way ahead would lead to the kitchens, eventually, but the hall shooting off to the right would lead to my private chambers. To my bed. To sleep.

I raised one hand, massaging my temples with my fingertip and thumb. When my eyes met Garath's, his filled with gentle hope, I couldn't help but think back to Hills's advice. I almost said yes. Almost.

With a sigh, I shook my head. "I'm sorry, Garath, but I'm exhausted," I told him. "Rain check?"

Garath's smile faded. "Yeah, sure." He turned away from me, but before he could take a step, I grabbed his wrist. His eyes met mine, his eyebrows climbing in question.

Acting on impulse, I stepped closer, rising onto my tiptoes. I pressed my lips to his cheek, and when I pulled away, he looked at me, and my stomach did a little flip-flop. His eyes searched mine, filled with questions. With hope. With desire.

Clearing my throat, I took a step backward, putting some much-needed distance between us. My heart hammered in my chest. I looked at Garath but quickly averted my gaze to the floor. "I'll, um, see you later," I said, risking one final glance at him before spinning around and hurrying down the adjoining corridor.

The whole way to my chambers, I fought the urge to turn around and run after Garath. Three more corridors and two flights of stairs weren't enough to bury the urge. But my desire for sleep was stronger, and by the time I reached the door to my rooms, it was all I could think about.

The moment I laid my hand on the doorknob, the whispers burst to life in my head.

Groaning, I rested my forehead against the door. There would be no chance of restful sleep now. Which meant I had to figure out what the whispers wanted me to do—and quickly—or I would be pulling another all-nighter.

I released the doorknob and turned my back to the door, looking up the corridor one way, then down the other, back the way I had come. The whispers seemed to be louder when I looked in that direction, so I sighed and turned to retrace my steps, heading down the staircase to the floor below.

The whispers led me to the double doors barring my mother's private study. Light seeped out from under the doors, and as I approached, the whispers gave way to real voices.

Masking my mind from others was second nature, so there was little chance of Mother detecting me lurking out in the hallway. But she wasn't deaf, so I slowed as I drew near, tiptoeing the final dozen steps to the doors. When I reached her study, I drew in a deep breath, held it, and leaned in, angling my ear toward the smooth panel of wood. The whispers quieted enough that I could hear the conversation taking place within the study clearly.

". . . never experienced anything like this before with a Healer," Mother said, her voice laden with exasperation. "It just doesn't make any sense!"

"Perhaps he is more than a mere Healer," a man said. I recognized the voice as belonging to Advisor Maylar, the royal spymaster. "Perhaps there is some Empath or Gauge in his blood. Then he would be able to guard his mind. After all, we've seen more muddled Abilities in Healers before . . ."

"That's impossible!" Mother snapped. "Stop speaking nonsense, Maylar. Jake is an original. His Ability is perfectly pure and untainted by interbreeding. It's the reason we need him."

"As you say, my queen," Advisor Maylar said, and I had a clear mental image of the man doubled over in his usual groveling bow. "Apologies. He is the oldest Healer we've ever encountered, and he's been dealing with Empaths since the very beginning. Perhaps he has built up some resistance to the Ability, or perhaps Zoe herself worked with him on creating this mental barrier."

There was a pause in the conversation, and ever so gently, I pressed my ear to the door.

"Perhaps it doesn't matter," Advisor Maylar continued. "*Perhaps* the solution is right under our noses. There is one his barrier could not possibly keep out. The princess need only touch him, and—"

"Out of the question!" Mother barked, the full power of her

position reverberating in her voice. "Princess Delphinia is to know nothing of this, or of the experiments at the prison, or of the malady plaguing the kingdom's elite. I prefer not to tarnish her tender heart with this ugly business."

My brows drew together, and my lips parted. Mother rarely showed so much emotion around me. I hadn't thought she cared about me as a person; I was merely another pawn to her. An heir to carry on her legacy.

"Besides," Mother continued, "we don't need his mind, we only need his blood. *He* is the true prize."

There was another pause in the conversation, and I held my breath, hoping it would continue.

"Oh, for the Patrons' sake," Mother said, "speak your mind Maylar, or surely you will explode from the effort of holding your tongue."

Maylar made a simpering noise, and my lip curled in disgust.

"He may know of other Healers of his generation," Maylar said. "If his pure blood truly is the key, would it not speed up the production process to have others like him, rather than to wait for his body to regenerate the lost blood?"

I heard a sigh, and I was fairly certain it belonged to Mother.

"Let us see what comes of the experiments," Mother said. "I'll spend the day tomorrow attempting to penetrate his mind, and you may oversee his transfer to the prison the following morning. If the preliminary tests show promise, then we may, once again, discuss the possibility of approaching Princess Delphinia. But if we do, we shall do so on my terms, and in my way. I cannot risk driving her away. She is the future of this kingdom."

"And yet," Maylar said, "if we don't find a permanent solution soon, the kingdom may be no more . . ."

With that, the whispers died out, and weariness washed over me like a warm blanket. Whatever I was supposed to hear, I had heard, though I was too exhausted to make sense of any of it right now.

Ever so slowly, I backed away from the door. I snuck back to my chambers, first tiptoeing, then running. But when I reached my rooms, I felt too wired to sleep. I paced around the dark sitting room, gnawing on my thumbnail as questions whirled around in my head.

What did it all mean? Why were the whispers leading me to all of these things—to Zoe's book, to Jake, to the map, and to Mother's study? Why was Jake so important to Mother? She needed his blood—but for *what*? Why was the kingdom in danger? And *what* was going on at the prison?

My sleep-deprived mind could only draw a single conclusion: I had to go to the prison to see for myself.

Determination took root within me. Tomorrow night. I would sneak out of the castle grounds and figure out some way to get to Prison Island and back before my absence was noticed. I didn't know how, but I trusted the whispers would aid me when necessary. After all, they had gotten me this far.

Sid shuffled along his perch in the corner of the room, fluffing his wings and cocking his head to the side. "Incoming!" he croaked, warning me that he could hear someone moving in the hallway.

It was probably just Mother heading to her chambers, but I wasn't willing to risk it. I fled into the adjoining bedroom and slipped under the covers. Just as I rested my head on the pillow, I heard the creak of the door from the hallway to my sitting room opening. I listened, breath held, as the intruder crossed to the bedroom doorway.

"Delphinia?" Mother said, her voice little more than a whisper. "Are you awake?"

I gasped, pretending I had startled awake, and rolled onto my back, blinking at her with bleary eyes. I watched Mother approach, her slight form a mere shadow in the dim light from the fireplace. She was a small woman with the presence of a giant.

She sat on the edge of the bed, her back to me, her long, dark curls cascading down her back. Her delicate profile appeared ageless in the darkness. She made no move to touch me like I imagined a loving mother might do. But then, Mother never touched me. At least, not on purpose. Touching me came with too many strings. Too many doors opened for me to glimpse behind. I was the most dangerous person in the kingdom to Mother. The most dangerous, and the most necessary.

"Hills stopped by my study after your training session," Mother said, her hushed voice a knife slicing through the silence. "She told me training didn't go well this evening . . . that you didn't seem yourself." Mother said no more, and after the silence stretched on for too long, I realized she was waiting for me to respond.

"I'm fine," I told her, then cleared my throat. "There's just a lot on my mind right now."

Mother inhaled deeply, exhaling in a sigh. She bowed her head slightly, her shoulders drooping. Another uncomfortable stretch of silence filled the room.

"I know you aren't looking forward to doing your part during the Bicentennial Celebration," she finally said, raising her head once more, "but our people will be looking to you to set an example of positivity and hope for the future. Seeing you settled and ready to continue the Corvo line will put their fears to rest. Our family is the backbone of the kingdom, and without us, everything our ancestors built would crumble. You are different from your subjects. Your life is not yours: it is theirs. Without them, you are nothing."

I bristled, hating the truth in her words. "I know, Mother," I said, my voice sounding hollow. "I will do my duty."

"But you won't like it," Mother mused. "Yes, well, neither did I."

She rarely spoke of Father, even in passing reference. He had died shortly before I was born, and not even my royal ears had been spared the whispered rumors of Mother's part in his death. It had never really bothered me—growing up without a father. Men weren't valued in the Corvo line. They were tools, a means to an end. Regardless, I had always wondered if there was any truth to the rumors surrounding Father's untimely demise. Though, of course, I'd never asked.

"But we do what must be done," Mother added, "no matter the cost."

I thought of my mission tomorrow, of the prison and Jake and the whispers. Of the secrets Mother was hiding from me.

"Yes, Mother," I agreed, my resolve hardening. "No matter the cost."

6

FIN

I'd woken with the sunrise, sleeping far longer than I'd intended, but there was nothing I could do about it. I wouldn't get to use the cover of night to my advantage, which meant I needed other means to get into the city.

I stared at the city walls a quarter mile out from my lookout, high up in a giant cypress. My mind was fresh from sleep, and I could easily null the guards whose mind signatures I felt at the parapet walk. Beast paced below, keeping an eye out while I focused all of my mental capacity on the city that towered ahead. From what I could see, the castle was bigger and more breathtaking than I'd expected it to be—the dark helm of a lost world at the edge of the ocean, and a beacon of hope for the people who didn't know any better.

The outer wall that surrounded the city was too tall to see much else. There were ways around that, though. Feeling the mind of a friendly flier above, I peered up through the branches into the sky. I linked with a red-tailed hawk as it flew in from the coast. Her belly was full from a morning hunt as she soared over the forest, the wind blowing through her feathers. Her eyes narrowed in on me through the tree canopy, and I felt her focus lock on me a moment before I was looking out through her eyes. She knew I was there, flying with her, and she didn't seem to mind in the slightest. *Friend.* It was a feeling we shared, more than a thought.

The city. I thought of its tall walls and willed Hawk to keep flying, past her nest and eggs on top of an abandoned building in the ruined cityscape, toward the fortress I was trying to break into. Happily, she did, her eyes shifting from me to the city of gray and white that gleamed in the morning light.

As the sun rose higher, life rustled within the city walls. With hawk eyes so keen, I could see people coming out of their shanty homes nearest the walls and the guards switching posts, like little ants in a maze. Smoke billowed from chimneys. Horses and carts cluttered the cobbled streets, and the main gates began to open for a day of trading. And when the hum of voices reached my ears through the whisper of the wind, I knew the city was waking up and it was the perfect time to join them.

As Hawk flew farther, I noticed two more walls separating the plebs in the shanty houses from the more stately manors and gardens that stretched out beyond them. A bell tolled ahead, and Hawk's eyes shot up from the view below. There it was, a hulking castle of dark stone, embellished with copper-capped turrets and flags flying on its pinnacles—ravens, obsidian black and taking flight. The Corvo family crest.

Hawk landed on a copper finial on the tip of the bell tower and stared down at the castle courtyard, where tents were being assembled. Men and women busied themselves, moving poles and banners, and pieces of a platform were being carried into place at the mouth of the gardens. They were preparing for a celebration or ceremony of some kind. Good. A celebration would draw in outsiders. That gave me one more excuse to get inside the walls of the city, and perhaps closer than I'd hoped was possible.

Hawk glanced around, surveying the rest of the bailey. The

castle boasted lush gardens with a rainbow of blossoms and rows of produce to the east, and stables and what looked like army barracks were situated to the west; barracks that easily housed dozens of guards, rangers, and knights.

The castle was surrounded by water and eucalyptus, and the grounds beyond stretched all the way to the sea. A high stone wall surrounding the castle grounds was the final barrier separating the Corvo family from the rest of the world.

Walls. Moats. Guards and armies. The royal family clearly worried for their safety, and they likely thought themselves elevated so far above everyone, they made sure to keep themselves well removed for that reason too.

The way the royals lived compared to the rest of the world was enough to stoke my hatred for them, and it burned like an ever-present brand. The royals had all of this, and still, they needed more? They needed Jake? For what? I had to quell the thought of burning everything to the ground once I was inside, knowing Jake had to be in the castle somewhere. If they wanted him so badly, they wouldn't risk taking him anywhere else—he'd been on the run for years and was nearly impossible to capture.

With a thought of gratitude toward my feathered friend, I blinked and my mind untethered from Hawk. Conviction renewed, I scaled back down the tree and landed on the forest floor with a thud.

Beast looked up from sniffing a mole hole in the ground, waiting for the verdict.

I stared at him, my chest tightening. I couldn't ignore the fact that taking Beast inside was impossible. We would stand out too much, and they might hurt him, which meant there was only one thing I could do. But leaving Beast behind might also mean I would never see him again.

As he realized my intentions, Beast trotted over to me. Reluctantly, I crouched down to say goodbye. He was more than a friend. He felt like a brother to me; we were connected in a way

I'd never been with any other living soul. His forehead met mine, his purr reverberating through his touch, as if he was reassuring me.

"I'll be back," I told him. "I promise." But even if I was determined to find out what was going on behind those walls and return home to my sister, either with Jake or with a plan, that didn't mean I would, and Beast knew it. "Give me a couple days," I told him. "Then go home to her, okay?"

Beast licked the scruff on my stubbled face in answer, then he growled at me to go find Jake.

With a heavy exhale, I rose to my feet, stashed my bow and quiver in the brush beside the tree for later, and pulled the balled up furs from my pack. The weight against my back lightened instantly with only the water in my deerskin and the few scraps of food left inside. I shook the tethered fox furs out and draped them over my shoulder to finish the effect. Then, I donned my cap and felt for my knife sheathed on my belt. There was no way the guards would let me into the city armed with my bow, so the small knife would have to do.

I looked at Beast one last time. He flicked his tail and yowled a goodbye, and I turned and headed toward the city walls. The gates were open, which meant they were expecting someone, or maybe a lot of someones for the celebration they were preparing for.

Pushing Beast's consciousness to the back of my mind, I focused on nulling myself as I approached the open gates. They were a couple of stories high, and a watchtower and battlement stretched out on either side. The gate itself was giant and slated with redwood planks, probably as thick as the trunks of the trees themselves.

As I drew closer, the forest thinned, and I noticed a few merchants making their way toward the entrance, forming a line to get into the city. My heart beat faster. A line could be good, or it could be bad.

I looked at the battlements once more, scanning for potential trouble. As confident as I was that I could bullshit my way out of just about anything, I was still wary. For all I knew, the guards would burn out my eyes if I looked at them wrong, or worse, they could throw me in jail and I would be useless to Jake.

I felt a couple of dozen minds scattered throughout the watchtowers and across the battlements, but with the onslaught of merchants making their way inside, I wasn't worried about the guards stretched out above as much as I was worried about the ones I was about to meet face to face.

It was hard to stay focused with all the people trickling in from the villages and farms throughout the kingdom. It was strange and exciting to see so many strangers for the first time in my life, and along with my awe and intrigue, I welcomed the bustle. I could barely fathom a life in the open, not having to hide because of the family you were born into.

With the gate only a dozen yards ahead and the hope of finding Jake so close, I wondered what the celebration was for, and if they'd taken Jake *because* of it. Had it been a witch hunt? Were they going to *try* to kill him for everyone to see? Was he a prize of some sort? A sacrifice?

I stopped behind an old man in the entrance line. His mule was pulling a wooden cart of wine barrels. I could smell the fermented grapes and sulfur. If the guards weren't mere feet in front of me, I would've considered reappropriating one of the half-barrels to steady my nerves before potentially locking myself within the walls with the people who were hunting my family.

Hearing a hum, I glanced over my shoulder. Two girls and a man sitting in an electric carriage, unlike anything I'd ever seen, rolled closer. It was hammered metal, with large, copper-spoked wheels patinaed by time. The driver turned the leather-lined steering disk with his gloved hands, and his wide foot eased off a flat petal, bringing the carriage to a stop behind me. Immediately, the electric hum ceased, and the two girls on the cushioned bench seat beside him giggled as they peered around, the jewels they wore glinting in the sunlight.

I glanced from the electric carriage back to the wine merchant's cart, noting the elevated difference of both merchants.

"Maybe we'll meet the princess this time, Papa," the younger of the girls said. Her dress was fine and fit for a well-bred lady, though she looked to be only ten years old.

Her father muttered something under his breath, which sounded a lot like, "Patrons help us if we do," and I couldn't help but feel validated in my hatred for the royals even more; even the more elevated commoners seemed unimpressed with their Corvo rulers.

"You won't meet the princess, stupid," the other girl said. "It's *her* celebration."

"It could happen," the younger girl bit back, and she opened her emerald-fringed parasol with a huff.

I rolled my eyes as they began to bicker back and forth. At least now I had an idea of what the celebration was for.

I tuned the girls out and focused ahead, noticing the mechanical levers that opened and closed the heavy gates and the giant crossbows that lined the ramparts. The castle was well equipped, and not just with Abilities.

The winemaker nudged his mule onward, and his wobbly wheeled cart lurched into motion and passed through the gates.

I was next.

Holding my breath, I stepped up to the guard, feeling a rush of panic and blood-boiling hatred as I took in his familiar, black leather armor. He wore a hammered, copper-plated helmet over his head, and a steel-hilted sword was strapped to his back. His mind radiated strength, but I pushed it away.

With dark, beady eyes and a pock-marked face, the guard scoured me up and down. He might not have been a ranger from the forest, but he was one of the queen's guards nonetheless, and I hated him. I gritted my teeth, feeling my jaw ache in response.

"What's your business in the city?" the guard barked and nodded to my pack.

"The celebration," I told him, trying to make my voice as even as I could manage.

"You and everyone else," he muttered and nodded to a line of merchants that weaved its way through the cobblestone streets behind him. There were dozens of them inside already, both with electric carriages and horse-drawn carts alike. "Everyone is trying to make a pretty penny on the Bicentennial Celebration," he grumbled and glanced at the guard assessing another visitor a few yards from me on the other side of the entrance.

They both rolled their eyes, and then the guard in front of me looked through my pack, seeing only my furs and what was left of my food. Next, he patted me down for weapons, feeling my knife sheathed at my side. Good. I wasn't trying to hide anything. I was only there to sell furs. *And to get a good look around and possibly free the queen's most valuable prisoner.*

The guard looked at my piddly knife and eyed me carefully. "You look young for a fur trader."

I shrugged, glaring at him as if I didn't appreciate his prying. "Ferals killed my pa when I was younger," I told him. It wasn't a lie.

The mention of Ferals had the guard dipping his chin with understanding. He didn't keep my knife, like I expected he would, either. Instead, he handed it back to me with a flash of sympathy crossing his features. Good, the people of Corvo City hated Ferals, or perhaps feared them, which meant I knew one more thing about them than I did before.

The guard was about to let me pass when he reached for my shoulder. "What's your Class, kid?"

I hadn't expected him to ask that, but then, since I was nulling him, he *would* be overly curious.

I nodded toward the seagull perched on the wall. "Telepathy," I told him honestly, though I left out the rest. With my beckoning, the seagull jumped from the wall and took flight, swooping down so far the guard cowered slightly in its shadow.

He glared at me, and I smiled. The gull seemed to be proof enough, and with a grunt, the guard let me pass. "If you want to set up a booth at the Bicentennial Celebration, registration is over there," he said, nodding to a line of merchants again. "They'll tell you when and where you can set up for next week's festivities."

I nodded in understanding.

"Move along now, kid," the guard said, waving the next merchant closer.

With a final glance over my shoulder in Beast's direction, I stepped into the mouth of the city, instantly assaulted by the scent of piss, stale beer, and manure. I wasn't in the mouth of the city, but the bowls of it.

Swallowing the bile that threatened to rise up my throat, I pushed my way through the merchants waiting in line to make a measly penny at the festivities and stopped where the alleyways parted, like three forks in a river.

Unlit street lamps lined the roads. A dog with a mangy fur coat sniffed an empty, discarded basket, his tail wagging as he moved on, trotting farther down the dirty street. Chickens flapped their wings and squabbled, broom bristles scraped against cobblestones, and people chatted at produce booths and called down from two-story windows. The buildings down here weren't exactly hovels, but they weren't like the homes I'd seen farther up the hillside. These people were the backbone of the city, yet they lived in the stench of poverty.

I was about to choose a path to follow, then stopped when I realized there were bends and alleyways that diverted in all directions. It truly was a labyrinth, and I could either waste time in alleyways of piss and chaos, or I could enlist the help of someone who knew the city better than me.

I made eye contact with a shepherd dog as it languidly walked past as if it was just another day. He stopped when he saw me, his head tilted to the side, and asked if I needed help.

I needed to gather more information about the supposed Bicentennial Celebration before I let the shepherd dog lead me deeper into the city. Information like what, exactly, was going to happen at the celebration and when it was taking place. I needed to know just how much danger Jake was in and how fast I needed to move.

Stinky, drunk men falling on their faces. I told the dog.

The dog understood my question well enough, and with a yip and a wagging tail, he began trotting down the middle alleyway, toward a tavern. Not only would I find out more about the celebration and the royal family's intentions, but I had a guide to the city, and for what felt like the first time since I forced myself to walk away from Jake, I allowed myself to breathe in relief. I was so close. I just needed a little bit more time.

7

DEL

I arranged the final pillow on the bed, then pulled the covers over all four of them and took a step back, planting my hands on my hips. My mouth quirked to the side as I assessed my work. Even better than last time. The wig was a nice touch.

I shifted my focus to the raven perched atop the back of the armchair angled toward the fireplace. Sid had been watching me arrange the pillows just so for the past fifteen minutes.

"Well, what do you think?" I asked him.

Sid cocked his head first one way, then the other, both of his beady onyx eyes focusing on me in turn. He hopped along the length of the chairback, fluffing his wings excitedly as he cawed. "Adventure time!" he croaked.

My hands slipped from my hips, and guilt blossomed in my chest. "No, Sid," I said, approaching the armchair. "You have to stay here this time." I almost never went anywhere without him, but then, that was the point of leaving him behind. "I'm sorry, but nobody's going to believe I'm a servant if I'm walking around with a raven on my shoulder."

I held my arm out toward him, and Sid hopped onto my fore-

85

arm, his partially outstretched wings softening the landing. I winced as his talons dug into my unprotected skin. He was being careful—he was always careful when I wasn't wearing my protective leather bracers—but it still hurt.

But just like bringing Sid with me out on my mission to sneak across the city and onto Prison Island would make me far too recognizable, so would my usual raven-ready attire. I had snuck a set of servants' livery from the laundry room earlier in the day, and I was hoping the tunic and pants of fine-woven charcoal cotton and black leather would help me blend in better. The raven insignia embroidered over the heart in silver thread marked me as a royal servant, but hundreds of Corvo City's citizens wore identical outfits every day. The white band encircling the crest labeled me a Telepath—close enough.

With Sid perched on my forearm, I started toward the doorway to the sitting room. "I really am sorry," I told him. "I'd much rather have you with me."

Once we were in the sitting room, I headed for the raven stand in the corner. I usually left the nearest window open for Sid to slip in and out of during the night, but I couldn't risk it tonight. He was too sneaky. Too loyal. If I didn't stop him, he would follow me.

I held my forearm out toward the raven stand, and Sid hopped onto the rail. I squatted down a little, placing my hands on my knees and looking the raven in the eye. "Stay here, Sid," I told him. "I mean it."

"Stay!" Sid croaked, then ruffled his feathers. "Good boy!"

I narrowed my eyes at him, wondering if ravens were capable of sarcasm.

With a sigh, I turned away, heading for the breakfast table. I grabbed the leather satchel propped up on my usual chair and set it on the table. I flipped the bag's flap open and double-checked the contents, making sure I had everything I thought I would need—waterskin, jerky, full-to-bursting coin purse, pistol, electric torch, leather gloves. My favorite set of daggers were tucked into the hidden sheaths in my boots.

I shut the bag and cinched the buckle, then slung it over my shoulder. I lifted the cloak from the back of the chair, settled it on my shoulders, and raised the hood over my head. There were a hundred other things I *could* bring with me, but more gear meant more weight and slower movement. Besides, my coin purse held plenty of money, and everyone knew that money could solve almost any problem.

I crossed the room, heading for the door. After one last glance at Sid, sulking atop his perch in the corner, I opened the door and slipped out into the hallway.

First, I looked up and down the corridor to make sure I was alone, and then I closed my eyes and focused on my mental barrier. I wasn't a Gauge. I couldn't affect others' Abilities, but I *could* alter others' mental impression of me. I could make myself undetectable. In a psychic sense, I was invisible.

I used the secret passages to move through the castle unseen, then slipped out through a servant's entrance in the kitchen. Workers were still cleaning up from the evening meal, and I had to keep my head down, my face hidden within the shadows of the cloak's hood.

Once I was outside, I skulked between the scattered bushes and trees surrounding the castle, then paused in some bushes to scope out the bridge. There was not a doubt in my mind that the bridge was being monitored, both psychically and visually. Psychically, I could handle. It was the actual eyeballs on the bridge that posed more of a problem. I could see only two options to make my way across—either swim underneath the bridge or crawl across it, concealed by the shadows lining the far edge. Seeing as I wasn't excited about the prospect of spending the rest of the night in wet clothes, I decided on the latter.

It was surprisingly degrading, crawling across the bridge, fear drumming a staccato beat in my chest. But I made it, and once I was hidden within the shadowed safety of the lush foliage on the far side of the gravel road, I brushed off my knees, and my pride made a full recovery.

Sticking to the deepest, darkest shadows, I snuck through the grounds, heading for the eastern escape passage. One had been built in each cardinal direction to allow for the queen and heir's escape, should the castle complex ever be breached.

It was still a couple of hours before midnight—late enough that there was no reason for anyone to be out here. I moved more freely, using trees for cover in case any of the telepathic guards were scouting the grounds through their raven's eyes. So far as I could tell, the only creature to have spotted me was a curious owl, perched in a tree near the waterfall.

I headed for the strategically laid path of stones jutting out of the water along the base of the rocky face over which the waterfall flowed, but I paused before setting my foot on the first stepping stone. I glanced back at the owl, my eyes narrowing in consideration as I chewed the inside of my cheek. There was a chance that the bird was a Telepath's familiar—a very small chance. Nonhuman telepathy was a rare skill valued by the castle guard, and all the guards who were able to communicate with animals used ravens to scout the castle grounds.

I wasn't one to condone violence against animals—ever—but I was even less willing to reveal the entrance to the eastern passage to some mysterious Telepath if indeed a person was watching me through the owl's eyes. Acting on a hunch, I picked up a small rock and chucked it at the bird.

My aim was true, and the owl took off in a burst of wings and feathers, just barely dodging the stone.

While the owl was distracted, I hurried along the path the stones cut through the water, heading straight for the waterfall. I slipped behind the falls, the spray dampening the right side of my cloak, and hurried into the tunnel chiseled through the bedrock, reaching into my bag for the electric torch as I went.

Mother had shown me the passages on my tenth birthday, the same day my training with Hills began. The same day I was deemed strong enough to be named the official Corvo heir. It had been far from a sure thing, me becoming the heir. When I was born, I was the youngest of four girls, but my two eldest sisters had slowly been picked off—assassinated in one way or another—until only Selestia and I remained. Selestia was the most like Mother in her Empathy. She had survived as the Corvo heir for eight years, only to be poisoned one week before the suitors were to arrive for the blood rites and her consort was to be chosen.

That left only me.

The tunnel felt smaller now. Cramped and closing in. The soft, golden light from the electric torch seemed to make the shadows beyond its reach denser and darker. Each footstep echoed up and down the tunnel, tricking my mind until I began to question whether or not I was actually being followed.

I picked up the pace, going from a fast walk to an easy jog, not wanting to spend any more time down here than was necessary. By the time I reached the exit—a dried-up well tucked away on the grounds of the Silva family estate—my breathing was labored and sweat beaded on my forehead and on the back of my neck.

I slowed to a walk as I approached the bottom of the well, then stopped and gazed up through the narrow, circular chute toward the dark, overcast sky. I angled the electric torch upward, examining the first few footholds carved into the well's interior wall, memorizing their placement before shutting off the light and returning the electric torch to my bag. I exchanged it for the leather gloves, then moved closer to the wall and started to climb.

My arms were trembling by the time I reached the rim of the well. With a grunt, I hoisted myself over and tumbled out onto the soft turf lining the ground. For long seconds, I simply lay there, catching my breath and second-guessing myself. But by the time my heartbeat slowed to a more comfortable pace, my worries had settled, and my resolve was back in place. I *had* to know what was going on at the prison.

With a deep breath, I stood and removed my gloves, tucking them into the bag as I scanned my surroundings.

The grounds of the Silva estate were lush and highly manicured, surrounded by a sturdy stone wall ten or twelve feet high. The manor house stood tall at the northern edge of the property, a small castle of stone, all the windows dark. A few gas lamps lit the exterior walls.

I jogged across the grounds, heading for the easternmost stretch of wall. Beyond it lay the less wealthy, more densely populated portion of the inner city. It would be strange to see a cloaked figure skulking about the avenues among the grand estates, but on the other side of that wall, where some people would still be out and about, I would blend right in.

Or so I hoped.

When I reached the wall, I ran my hands along its disappointingly smooth surface. I wouldn't find any good hand or footholds, so climbing wasn't an option. But an oak tree closer to the manor house had a sturdy looking branch that stretched out over the wall.

Grinning to myself, I jogged to the oak and quickly donned my gloves once more as I studied the trunk for the best route up. I had been quite the tree-climber as a kid, and though I hadn't attempted to scale a tree in years, I found it came back to me easily enough. I climbed up to the branch that extended over the wall and paused to catch my breath. It didn't look nearly as sturdy from up here, and I suddenly felt far less certain about this plan.

But I had come this far. There was no point in turning back.

One deep breath later, I was balancing on the branch, one foot in front of the other, my arms stretched out to either side. I stepped carefully, moving slowly. The branch creaked and swayed as I made my way farther from the trunk.

At the sound of an ominous *crack*, I leapt from the branch and clung to the top of the wall, my legs dangling precariously down toward the grounds of the Silva estate. Grunting and cursing, I clambered up onto the top of the wall and huddled there for a solid minute, waiting for the trembling to cease and for my nerves to regroup.

I took slow, deep breaths as I studied the paved avenue on the other side of the wall in the dim light of the gas street lamps. The far side of the road was lined by a string of several-story buildings, all with dark windows, which I was grateful for, but the road below me was lined with manicured hedges and thorny rose bushes. Hardly an ideal landing pad. A ways up the wall, the road curved away, leaving room for a park-like expanse of grass that would do nicely.

I stood, crouching to stay low, and snuck along the top of the wall toward the grassy area. At the *hoot hoot* of an owl, I froze. Then I gave up on sneaking and ran along the top of the wall, scrambling down and dropping onto the cushioned lawn. I rolled to break my fall, but quickly regained my footing and ran across the road to duck into a dark alleyway between two stretches of buildings.

This part of the inner city housed the wealthier merchants and tradespeople and was laid out in a clean grid that followed the original city's ancient footprint. I needed only to pick an east-west running road and follow it a couple of dozen blocks until I reached Market Street. Then it would be a straight shot to the docks, where I could bribe a fisherman into ferrying me to Prison Island.

I peered back at the wall surrounding the Silva estate. There was no way I would be able to scale the wall unnoticed from the outside. After all, the whole point of the wall was to keep people out, and there were no conveniently placed trees.

I would need to use another passage to return. An inconvenience, more than anything. This passage was the most direct shot to the harbor . . . and to Prison Island. The northern passage would have to do. It would mean more time spent navigating a more heavily patrolled portion of the inner city, but there wasn't much to be done about it.

I looked down the alleyway and was pleased to find that it ran the whole way through the block. As I watched, a few people passed by the far mouth of the alley. Likely servants for the grand estates, either running some late-night errands or heading home. Almost all the passersby wore cloaks just like mine. I grinned. My plan to blend in would work!

I started down the alley, moving off to the right side as a man entered from the far end. I kept my face angled downward but watched him in my peripheral vision.

When I was about to pass the man, he started toward me. "Hey—" His voice was low and rough.

Fear spiked within me. I turned around, intending to flee and take the long way around the block, but a large dog barred the way, his head hanging low and menacingly. They had trapped me.

He could be an assassin or just a random thug. It didn't really matter. I struck without warning, and the man backpedaled as he attempted to deflect my blows. He was surprisingly quick, and his attempts to dodge me were effective. Not a thug, then. Was he really an assassin here to take out the last remaining princess? He had training. He knew how to handle himself in a fight.

I didn't let up, backing him against the wall of the alley. Between a kick and a jab, I drew the knife from my left boot and held the razor-sharp edge flush against his throat.

He stilled, a trickle of blood streaking down the front of his neck. If he moved, he was dead.

"What do you want?" I hissed, raising my right hand to press it against the side of his face so I could read his mind.

Something slammed into the backs of my legs, and my knees gave out. I had forgotten about the damn dog. I stumbled to the ground, the dagger flying from my hand and clattering on the cobblestones far out of reach. I coiled my legs to lunge toward the weapon, but the dog stepped in my path. A low growl rumbled in his chest. I crouched there, my breath frozen in my lungs.

A heartbeat later, the man tackled me to the ground. "Hey—" he growled, and I was flattened out on my belly with an *oomph*. The man straddled my back, his hands pressing my wrists into the ground over my head. "Enough," he said gruffly.

I struggled, wriggling and grunting, but all it achieved was tiring me out, and I was no closer to breaking free. I fell still, breathing hard and heart pounding, panic slowly coiling in my gut.

My attacker leaned in close until I could feel his chest heaving against my spine and his breath hot against the back of my neck. "I don't want to hurt you," he said. "I need your help. I know you snuck off castle grounds, and I need you to sneak *me* in."

Curiosity wrestled with my panic, momentarily winning. I closed my eyes, diving into my attacker's mind, skimming all I could in a few seconds. I saw flashes of a woman with blonde, curly hair, and of a giant cat. Of a fight in the woods and scattered dead bodies. Of a man's face—Jake's face. My heart ached with my attacker's pain. He had lost so many, and he blamed the Corvo kingdom. Mother. Me. His hatred for my family ran bone-deep. And after all he had lost, I could hardly blame him.

Tears leaked from my eyes as I dove deeper into his mind, seeking out his connection to Jake. This man—Fin was his name —was here to rescue Jake. It was his first time in the city, and he wasn't going to leave without Jake.

But Fin didn't understand the bigger picture, and if I told him that Jake was a part of something more—if I told him how I knew, he would deduce who I was, and because of his hatred for my family, he would never trust me. But I needed him. He was clever and far more worldly than me. And his control over the animals could definitely come in handy during the night's risky mission.

This was a tricky situation, but there was a way I could use Fin's determination. A way I could harness his anger and hatred.

Pulling out from his mind, I thought of Adasia and how frightened she would be in a situation like this. I thought of her mannerisms and ways of speaking. I thought of her easy smiles and ready tears. Tears would do perfectly, and I didn't even need to fake it. Fin's heartache had been more than enough to trigger the waterworks.

I cleared my throat, and then I whimpered. "I can't do as you ask," I said, a tremble to my voice. "The princess sent me out on an urgent errand, and I must fetch her healing elixir from Prison Island undetected and return before sunrise, or she'll—she'll—" I sniffed and stuttered. "I don't think I'll survive another beating like that . . ."

Horror washed over me from Fin, followed by a rush of sympathy. My sniveling explanation had only fueled his hatred for the Corvo family. No matter. So long as he believed me to be a victim of his enemy, he would be more likely to help me.

Fin released my wrists, cutting off my connection to his mind. "I—I'm sorry. I had no idea," he said, moving off me. "Here, let me help you." He offered me his hand, his face set in a grim expression.

I pushed up to my hands and knees, then placed my hand in Fin's. I sensed it the moment he connected the misplaced dots— healing elixir and Prison Island—and surmised that Jake must be imprisoned there. A plan quickly formed in his mind. It was almost too easy.

Fin released my hand, but it was too late for him. I already knew I had him. "I can help you," he said, "with your errand, I mean. After frightening you like that, it's the least I can do."

I sniffed and wiped away the tears drying on my cheeks. "Thank you," I said, meeting his eyes. "I would really appreciate your help."

8

FIN

Per the servant girl's directions, we followed the gas-lit cobblestone roads a dozen or so blocks until Market Street came into view. Her footsteps were quiet compared to mine, but just as determined. She was on a mission, her fear of the princess fueling every hasty step. Good. I had a sickening suspicion I was running out of time, and now that I knew where they were keeping Jake and the healing elixir they must have been stealing from his blood, I figured this servant girl was my best hope—no, perhaps my *only* hope—to get to him.

The moon glistened off the harbor, and I used its light to guide us toward the dock. It would be easy enough to steal a boat in the cover of night, but it was getting back after I found Jake that would likely prove more difficult.

I glanced back at the servant girl, the shadows of night covering her face beneath her hood. "I'm Fin, by the way." A silver raven embroidered on her chest flickered in the moonlight.

"Ada," she said after a moment's hesitation. "And while I appreciate you helping me get to the prison, you might want to work on how you go about asking for help, you know, in case there's a next time."

I smirked and adjusted my pack on my back as the docks came into view. "I might've been able to if you hadn't tried to make a pancake of my face."

Ada's eyes flicked to mine and lingered. She still seemed uncertain of me after our brief grappling match, but I didn't blame her, even if she'd been the one to strike the first blow. Not only had I spied on her through wide owl eyes as she'd made her escape from castle grounds, but I was also a stranger trying to do the opposite and sneak *inside.*

But regardless of Ada's wary voice and the few paces she kept between us, one thing was certain—there was a fire inside of her and she could take care of herself. I had the dried blood on my throat to prove it.

I recalled her urgent errand for the princess. "What are you to the royal family?" I asked, glancing back at her. The road was dark and the castle distant behind us as we made our way down the hill.

The longer Ada remained quiet, the more uneasy I became, and I peered over my shoulder at her again. "I can't imagine a kitchen maid knows how to fight like that." My smile broadened at the thought, and I stopped in front of her, pinning her dark gaze with my own.

Ada's eyes shimmered in the moonlight beneath the hood of her cloak, but it wasn't with tears or what was left of them. This time her eyes shimmered with curiosity, or perhaps the sheer will to carry out her task as her princess commanded. I tried not to spit at the thought of her highness sitting up in her fancy tower while Jake was likely hanging from his ankles while the blood was being drained from him, or worse. "So, what are you, an armed lady-in-waiting or something?"

With a purse of her lips, Ada nodded. "Something like that." Her eyes narrowed on me ever so slightly, and I knew she wasn't telling the whole truth. With a defiant lift of her chin, she walked past me, her shoulder brushing mine as she continued toward the docks. Whatever she was, Ada was changeable. She'd been near tears only minutes ago, and now her face was a veneer of focus and resolve.

"So, the princess is surrounded by an army of her own then," I mused. If she had shieldmaidens willing to die for her, regardless of how horrid she sounded, I could only imagine the security measures taken with the queen, herself. "Wonderful," I muttered.

Ada gave me a sidelong look as I fell into step beside her. "You sound disappointed," she said, glancing from me back to the road. "I doubt you were trying to get inside to leave a bouquet of flowers on the princess' pillow. So why then?" I noted the sharp edge to her tone. "Were you trying to hurt her?"

"The princess?" I shook my head. "I hadn't even thought about her until you said something," I admitted. "But you don't paint a friendly picture of her," I added.

"You're trying to hurt someone else, then?"

Again, I shook my head. "I'm not going to lie, I would love to see the royal family burn in a hellfire of their own making, but I'm not here to kill anyone. I—" I stopped myself before I gave too much away.

I could feel Ada's gaze on the side of my face, but I ignored it. The less she knew, the better. She seemed to agree, and we remained silent for the rest of the walk through the shop-lined streets.

Windows were dark for the night, and smoke swirled steadily from chimneys, filling the air with the scent of burnt pine that commingled with the brine of the sea. It was a different world halfway up the hill where the merchants appeared to thrive, away from the dingy gutters of the lower city.

As we drew nearer to the harbor, I peered over the low stone wall that separated the city streets from the docks. The pier was a U-shaped port with a dock on either side that stretched out as far as I could see, lined with ships of all sizes.

The Bicentennial Celebration. It was a bigger deal than I'd originally thought, and like the merchants with their carts loaded with goods, mariners had come to call from all around as well. Longships and cargo vessels, unlike any I'd ever seen, lined the piers, their hulls made of black-veined, rich redwoods. Some had six sails, others had only one, and their masts and sails hung in all shapes, colors, and sizes.

"What is the Bicentennial Celebration?" I asked, curiosity getting the better of me. The crowded docks and streets couldn't have worked out better if I'd planned it all myself. "I know it's a festival celebrating two centuries of Corvo rule," I said. "But what's that got to do with the princess?" Once the men in the tavern had told me that the festivities were the largest in their lifetime, bringing together counties and villages from all over the kingdom, I'd stopped listening to the rest.

With a snide laugh, Ada looked me up and down, eyeing my buckskin tunic and trousers. I resituated my pack on my back, uncomfortable under the weight of her stare.

"You're clearly not from around here," she said with far too much amusement. "And you're obviously up to no good, so why would I tell you anything about the princess?"

It was a valid question, which only spurred another one of my own. "Why *wouldn't* you tell me? If your princess is so horrible—if you're so worried about being punished—why do you care what happens to her?"

The glint in Ada's eyes faded and she stared straight ahead. "She's not horrible," she said so quietly I could barely hear her. "And I don't know what it's like where you come from, but here we are duty-bound." There was a distinct longing in Ada's voice, though I wasn't sure what for. To be able to make her own choices? To rid herself of her duty to the kingdom and the princess?

"That's why I'm here," I admitted, feeling a sudden kinship with Ada. "A sense of duty, I guess."

Again, she looked at me, only this time, I met her gaze, knowing I couldn't trust her but wanting to all the same. "I told you, I'm not here to hurt the royal family. I'm here to find a friend."

A flash of something that looked a lot like sorrow or perhaps understanding lit Ada's face, and she cleared her throat. "For the princess, the festivities also mark the beginning of her engagement," she explained flatly, and I detected a little regret.

"Let me guess, he's a balding old guy that she hates?" I laughed at the thought. "Rough life," I muttered.

Ada's eyes fixed forward, and she shrugged. "She doesn't even know who he will be. She's never met any of the suitors who are coming to compete for her hand."

While I had no sympathy for the princess, Ada's forlorn expression left me without a quip or jab at the royal family's expense this time. And after a few awkward moments, I forced myself to refocus on the glow of a prison on the craggy rocks that jutted out of the bay on the horizon.

Prison Island. The structure was nestled in the cliffs and surrounded by a shadowy belt of trees. If I didn't suspect the possible horrors it housed, I might've even thought it was impressive, but I knew better than that. It was a stone fortress with a watchtower that stood like a javelin from the center of it. I tried not to let the uncertainty of what I would be walking into unsteady me, though the knot in my stomach tightened at the thought.

Ada and I turned the corner of an alleyway as we reached the edge of the city. The neighborhood opened up toward the wall surrounding the pier, with only a narrow road between us.

"Wait." I grabbed onto Ada's arm and pulled her back into the shadows of the stable on the corner. The owl was close, and while he sensed no significant threats, a few minds tingled on my periphery. Manure tinged the air, reminding me we were no longer in the pristine neighborhoods up the hill, and down here, minds stirred, drunk and restless. I cleared my throat. "You've been to the island before, right?"

"No, actually," Ada said, shaking her head reluctantly. Not a place for servants then, I gathered. At least not young, pretty ones who were meant to wander the lavish halls of a castle instead of the cold, dank stone halls of a prison.

I gritted my teeth and glanced out at the island again. *Damn.*

"What will we do?" Ada whispered, frantically glancing around.

"I'll come up with something," I told her. I had to.

Ada watched with confusion as I shrugged my pack off and pulled my fur cape out. I swung it over my shoulders and clasped it around my neck, once again donning the guise of the trapper who had gotten me into the city so convincingly.

"Clever," Ada muttered, and I saw another flash of amusement in her eyes.

I smirked to hide my uncertainty. I had no idea what I was doing, but then again, I always thought better on my feet. "I hope you ate a hearty dinner." I peered up at the cypress trees that bent in the evening wind. "That water is going to be choppy, and I'm going to need your help rowing." While stealing a sailboat to get us to the island would be far faster on a windy night like this, it would also be the most obvious, so a rowboat would have to do. Again. I groaned inwardly.

"I can do that," Ada said, tucking a dark curl back up into her hood. Her features were set with an adamant focus I admired. She pulled her woolen cloak tighter around her and straightened her back as if she were preparing for battle.

I smiled. "Good." Shrugging my pack on again, I took a quick mental scan of the surrounding minds. We didn't need unwanted attention, not when I was so damn close to finding Jake, so I nulled any guards and passersby.

A bark of laughter caught in the breeze, and Ada and I crouched down, dipping farther into the shadows. A guard in leather garb stepped into the open gate of the harbor entrance, though his attention was focused on the golden-haired woman in a rumpled blue dress he pressed up against the stone wall.

I felt three minds in the area, the woman and the guard, and another one that barely hummed with consciousness somewhere inside the walls. "They're drunk," I whispered, and as the woman began to lift her skirts, a crazy, yet necessary idea sparked to life.

I turned to Ada. "Do you trust me?"

She looked taken aback, but after a moment, she dipped her chin. "I suppose—"

"Good," I said in a rush. "Laugh like you've had too much mead, and follow my lead. You got it?"

As Ada began to nod again, her eyes wide and questioning, I laughed and grabbed her hand, tugging her out into the gas-lit street. She nearly faltered in my haste, looking the part of a stumbling drunk, and then her sweet laughter filled the air.

The guard lifted his head from the woman's neck and craned to look at us as we drew closer. He instantly scowled as he took in the sight of us. "What are you two doing out here?" he demanded, though his voice was hoarse and saturated with lust and booze.

When I realized Ada's laughter had subsided and she was turned away, trying to tug her hand from mine, I drew her closer and pressed a kiss to her mouth. Her body stiffened with shock, but she didn't have time to pull away before the guard shouted at us again.

"Hey—" He took a step closer.

I laughed, my heart hammering in my chest, and nodded toward the anchored ships. "We're just looking for a place to get away from her father," I explained with an oversized grin. "He's a better marksman than me." I winked at him.

When I glanced back at Ada, she had her back to the guard, and I worried she'd blow our cover. Pulling her against my chest,

I smirked at the guard, ignoring the booze that wafted off him. "She's unplucked," I muttered with hungry, hopeful eyes. "And I'm looking for some sport after weeks out at sea." I swayed on my feet for good measure, gripping Ada tighter to me, willing her to play her part. Eventually, she leaned her head against my shoulder, her face cast in the shadow of her hood.

The guard's eyes narrowed on Ada, the gas lamp shadows flickering across her.

"She's quite shy, as you can see," I whispered and leaned closer to the guard with dancing eyebrows. "But the best ones always are, right?"

"Oh, Farrrriiissss . . ." The woman cooed the guard's name, urging him back over to her. "My husband will wonder where I am." She pulled up her skirt a little, teasing him.

The guard glanced at Ada then at me once more, and with a curt nod, he flicked his gaze to the pier behind him. "If you get caught, I won't stop her father from maiming you," he warned.

"Fair enough," I said wryly, and pulling impatiently on Ada's hand, I tugged her past the guard, whose attention quickly shifted back to his companion.

As we hurried through the gatehouse entrance onto the pier, I tugged Ada past a few ships and out of earshot, not bothering to hide my impatience. The wood creaked beneath our feet, and I glowered at her as we finally stopped for breath . . . only to find her glaring at *me*.

She tore her hand from mine.

"What the hell was that?" We both asked at once.

I shrugged. "You wanted to get onto the docks, didn't you?"

"Not like *that*," she spat.

"Well, I had to come up with something. We're running out of time." My eyes narrowed on her. "Why did you turn away from him? You almost blew the whole thing." I was beginning to wonder if Ada wanted me to get caught.

"*Why?*" she practically seethed. "Because he would have

recognized me, you idiot." Her eyebrows lifted and just as suddenly, her shoulders straightened, and she composed herself again. "You think they don't know what the princess's ladies look like? We're only on parade every single day. If he'd seen me, he would've asked too many questions. He would have started snooping around, and this is a secret matter, *remember*?"

I felt my cheeks redden slightly. She was right. *I* could've ruined everything. But I didn't admit that to her. "Well, it worked, didn't it?" Squaring my shoulders, I turned on my heel and headed for the smaller boats at the end of the pier.

"Barely," she muttered as she fell into step behind me. "Has anyone ever told you you're reckless?"

"All the time," I said, glaring at the rowboats at the end of the pier as we drew closer.

"Well, do us both a favor, and next time you have a hair-brained plan, run it by me first."

I rolled my eyes as we reached a tiny old sailboat with a broken mast that wouldn't likely be missed.

"*That's* what we're taking?" Ada practically squeaked, incredulous. I followed her gaze to the rough waters beyond the pilings. "Is it safe?"

"I can't sail a ship on my own unless they taught you how to do that in your princess guard lessons?" I pointed for her to climb into our new rowboat while I stepped into another. We would need two sets of oars if we were going to get to the island before the sun began to rise, exposing us more than we already were.

With a sidelong look, Ada cautiously boarded the boat, clasping onto the sides as she steadied herself before stumbling onto the wood crossbeam at the stern to sit.

I bit back a smile as I grabbed an oar in each hand and climbed onto the pier again, wondering if Ada had ever been out of the city, let alone been in a boat in rough waters.

"Sit there," I told her, nodding to the center thwart at the rowlock. "It will be easier to control those oars since they're locked in place."

Ada grumbled as she braced herself on the edge of the boat. Once she was seated again, I climbed inside and took my place at the stern.

Ada was still glaring at me. "What?" I asked. "You're not still annoyed about that kiss, are you? I'm sorry, okay? It was a dumb idea. It's not like it was enjoyable or anything."

Her eyes narrowed to dagger tips, and I could practically feel them twisting into my soul.

I rolled my eyes. "You know what I mean."

"Can we please just get on with this?" she gritted out, and I ran my hand over my face with a sigh.

"Yeah. Okay." When I opened my eyes again, I saw a flash of unease in Ada's expression as she peered out at the water. She wasn't just angry with me, she was clearly nervous. "I know the waters are rough," I started, which was a bit of an understatement. Her hood whipped off in a sudden gale. "But we need to row together to make double-time and get through the whitecaps. It will be okay. I'm a great swimmer if you happen to fall in." Ada's eyes widened, and I winked at her. "You ready?"

Though Ada was clearly unsettled by what we were about to do, she pursed her lips and took a deep breath. "I'm ready."

At my request, she waited for me to guide us out of the harbor and around the other boats, out into open waters, then she fell into a rowing rhythm with me.

The wind was biting cold, and I was grateful for the furs that covered me.

Despite Ada's best efforts to tighten her hood around her face, it blew off again, and her shoulder-length, raven-black curls whipped out of her braid and around her face. Her features were delicate, and her tan skin wasn't weathered like so many of us from hard work back home. She looked soft and almost exotic, as if Ada was a breed of a special kind of nobility all her own. I wasn't sure I'd ever seen a girl quite like her in my life.

She shivered as water splashed up into the boat, and I heard Jake's voice in the back of my head, followed by Autumn's chastising. *"The least you can do after embarrassing her is give her your damn cloak."* Fleetingly, I wondered if Ada had ever kissed anyone in her life and if that was part of why she was so angry with me.

"What?" she snapped. "Why are you staring at me?" Her tear-stained cheeks from our tussle by the castle felt more and more like a joke as the crying, terrified girl I'd first met faded behind the bold, bristly warrior-in-waiting who sat across from me with a permanent scowl etched on her face.

"What's your Ability, anyway?" I asked her, ignoring her question. I knew it had to be something useful and important, or she wouldn't be in the princess's entourage.

Ada blinked at me and she licked her lips, like she wasn't sure she could trust me. She was right not to, just like it was becoming clear that I shouldn't trust her either. "You mean, my Class?"

I shrugged. "If that's what your people call it."

Her eyes narrowed. "What's yours?" she countered.

Shaking my head, I wondered how much to give this girl. While she was my ally now, there was no telling what would happen once she realized I was using her to get to Jake—to rescue the very source her princess needed for her precious elixir. My jaw twitched with resolve. "Telepath," I admitted.

"Animal?"

The owl. She'd known someone was watching her; it was why she'd thrown the rock at him in the first place. I dipped my chin in answer and continued rowing.

"Telepath," she finally revealed. "Not animals."

Unspoken and secret communications—it was a handy Ability for her princess, so it made sense.

We rowed in silence after that, both of us growing warier of one another by the minute. My arms flexed with fatigue after yesterday's journey across the bay, but at least the island was getting closer.

I turned the oars again and again, appreciating the way Ada attempted to keep up, though her white knuckles gave her away; she was exhausted and straining, but she wouldn't give up. That was at least one thing we had in common.

She peered past me, at the prison, as we drew closer to the island. "They're going to sense us coming," she said. "If they haven't already."

I wasn't worried about that. I was nulling them, just in case. "I'm more worried about finding an alternative way in since I assume walking through the gates isn't part of the plan."

"There are tunnels," she said. "Near the back. The royal family *loves* its secret passageways. I'm just not sure exactly where they are from here."

"Let me see if I can find them," I said, and swallowing thickly, I closed my eyes. "Keep rowing," I told her as my movements began to slow.

"What—"

Ada's words broke off, or maybe they just faded as my mind connected with the owl's again. He flew like a soaring arrow in the dark night, hovering over the island as he fixated on every twitching, weed stalk and crevasse for his prey. With a silent request to take over, I peered around the rock face, looking for the entrance to the tunnel system we could use to get inside unseen.

When I opened my eyes again, the icy wind hit my face, nothing like when I was flying as the owl. It wasn't liberating, but abrasive and painful. I shivered, blinked my eyes into focus, and found Ada's head cocked to the side, her attention fixed on me.

"I found the tunnel," I told her and began guiding the boat

around to the back of the island with more fervor. "Come on, we're almost there."

The island seemed enormous as the rough waters pulled us closer and closer to the rocky shore. "There—" I pointed to the passage.

"That . . . looks more like a sewer," she said and looked none too happy about it.

I grinned, wondering if she'd ever *really* gotten dirty in her life. I imagined defensive training within the castle walls hadn't prepared her for a moment quite like this. "What's the matter? Have you been hanging around the princess too long? Are you afraid to get a little dirty?"

Ada's surprise pinched into that ever-present glare of hers I was growing so fond of, and I refrained from a chuckle.

As the boat scraped and lurched against the rocks below, I jumped into the frigid water, my legs stinging as it splashed up to my knees. With a heave, I pulled the boat onto the shore, and to my surprise, Ada quickly jumped out to help me.

"If this floats away," I told her, pulling in a breath as I wrapped the rope a few times around my arm for leverage, "we're stuck here. We have to secure it up in these rocks in case the tide comes in."

Ada nodded, shivering, but the determination I'd seen in her eyes before shone brightly in the gleaming moonlight.

"On the count of three," I said, knowing this would be a lot harder than it looked. We were both tired from battling the waves and the wind. "Don't stop pulling," I told her. "One. Two. Three."

The frame of the boat creaked, we groaned, and with every single resolve-infused muscle, we pulled and pulled. The rocks scraped against the bottom slats, but finally, the stern was dragged up and out of the water entirely and rested between the stones.

Ada and I stumbled back, bracing ourselves against the cliffside. We looked at each other, trying to catch our breath. Despite Ada's secrets, she was made of tough stuff, and without her, I'd still be trying to figure out how to get into the castle, only to find Jake wasn't even there.

A small smile tugged at the corner of her mouth. "We did it," she rasped.

"Miraculously," I added with a smile of my own, and this time, when I noticed she was shivering, wet and windblown, I unclasped my fur cloak and wrapped it around her.

She eyed me skeptically.

"Don't overthink it," I told her.

Ada's eyes lingered on mine a moment longer before she sat up, pulling the cape tighter around her. "Thank you."

I nodded and brushing the sand and dirt off my sweaty hands, I stood and held out my hand to help her to her feet.

Ada was about to accept when she paused, hesitating for a moment before her fingers curled around mine. I tried not to think too much about her reluctance and climbed through the rocks toward the narrow metal-paneled door hidden in the shadows.

Ada was right; it didn't look very welcoming. The passage was clearly rarely used. The door, covered in cobwebs and bird poop, was completely rusted shut and forgotten. And if the size of the door was any indication, the tunnel would be a tight squeeze for the both of us.

I pulled my knife from my belt and stared at its thick blade. It was too big to pick a lock. I peered around, imagining a stone a bit larger than my fist might be able to bust it open.

"Here," Ada said, and she unclasped the buckle of her bag peeking out from beneath her two cloaks. She rustled around inside, then pulled out an electric torch and a pistol.

Luckily for me, the princess had sent her out more prepared than I was. I nodded to the rusted, locked door that separated me from Jake. "Well then," I prompted. "Would you like to do the honors?"

Without hesitation, Ada pointed the barrel of the pistol at the latch and pulled the trigger. For the first time all night, I was relieved there was a howling wind because, with a single gunshot that disappeared in the wind, the steel door squeaked open.

Ada flicked on the electric torch. Clever little device. And convenient. "You really were on a mission tonight," I mused.

Ada raised a dark, delicate eyebrow at me and smiled.

Feeling a strange sense of admiration for her, I scrubbed the back of my head and gestured toward the tunnel. "By all means, after you, tough stuff."

9

DEL

I held the electric torch out in front of me as Fin and I peered into the tunnel. The darkness was so heavy, it almost seemed solid. The walls of the tunnel bore deep groove marks, and the floor was slick with moss or algae, though it looked like it receded up ahead. The tunnel had a slight, almost imperceptible angle of ascent. The smell of the sea mingled with the cold stone, transforming into something dank and musty.

I wrinkled my nose and we started forward. The sound of the soles of my boots scuffing over the rock echoed deeper into the tunnel, and I made an effort to walk softer.

I glanced over my shoulder at Fin. He was following close behind me. "This used to be a temple, you know," I told him, my voice hushed. "The first queen converted it from a prison to a place of remembrance and worship devoted to the Patrons. That's when they added this tunnel, so the priests could escape if the temple was ever attacked." While I had never visited this place myself, I'd learned of the escape passage long ago. *This* escape passage.

"Worship . . ." Fin said derisively, laughing under his breath.

I glanced back at him once more to see him shaking his head. "Well, they turned it back into a prison," I said, feeling slightly defensive.

"You know your 'Patrons' were just people." Fin's words were little more than a whisper. "They were survivors like everyone else. They'd think you were crazy for worshiping them the way you do."

I frowned, furrowing my brow. It was a shocking thing to say. Heresy. None who lived within Corvo City would ever utter such words. Without the Patrons, our world would've been a very different place, ruled by Controllers manipulating the minds and bending the will of everyone around them. Making slaves of us all.

I peered back at Fin. Who was this man, really? My fingers itched to touch him again so I could delve deeper into his mind and learn more about who he was and where he came from. How exactly did he know Jake? Why did he care enough about Jake to risk his own life to save him? And why was he so certain the prison guards wouldn't sense us? Was he able to guard his mind the same way I could guard mine?

The need to know more became overwhelming, and I rounded on Fin.

He backed up a step, his hands partially upraised. "Whoa," he said. "What's up, tough stuff?"

"Who are you?" I asked, voice low and urgent. "And why aren't you worried about the guards sensing us?"

Fin tilted his head to the side, sizing me up. And then, unexpectedly, he smiled and bowed. "Finlay Cartwright," he said, "at your service."

I shook my head, my eyes narrowed, and studied Fin as he straightened. The Cartwright name. Red hair and green eyes, just like Dani. My eyes widened, and my lips parted. "You're a Ghost," I whispered, my hand covering my mouth.

Fin's eyebrows crept higher, and he looked down at himself, incredulous. "Pretty sure I'm alive," he said wryly.

Again, I shook my head. "Not that kind of ghost," I said, lowering my hand. "The Ghosts are a legend—a rumor. Something people whisper about in dark corners."

Fin smirked. "And who are these *Ghosts* supposed to be, according to your rumors?"

"They're the descendants of the Patrons," I told him. "They're of all Classes, wielding terrifying power that makes them more god than man. It's said they roam the wildlands to the north, searching for unsuspecting wanderers, and if they catch you, you vanish, never to be seen of or heard from again."

Fin's amusement faded and his cheek twitched. "Gods, eh?" he sniggered, an almost disgusted sound, and shook his head. "Interesting."

I took a single step closer to him, peering up into his eyes. His face was cast in the golden light from the electric torch, and his irises shone a haunting yellow-green. "So it's true, then?" I asked. "You're really one of them?"

Fin was silent for a moment as he studied my face, his eyes searching mine. Finally, he blew out a breath. "Dani and Jason Cartwright were my great-"—he raised a hand and started ticking off *greats* on his fingers—"great-great-great-great-great-*great*-grandparents," he admitted. "And as handy as godly powers would be, I just have a combination of both of their Abilities."

I took another step toward Fin, my eyes glued to his.

Fin broke our stare, looking away.

"And there are more of you?" I asked.

Fin's eyes snapped back to mine, his stare hardened by fear. "Yes," he said, the single word laced with heat and anger. "But we're not talking about them." He narrowed his eyes, and I could practically see the wheels turning behind those big green irises. He was assessing me, and I watched the distrust settle in his stare. Fin leaned closer, his jaw set as if he was challenging me to press him further. "Now, if you don't mind, I'd like to keep moving." He shot a pointed look beyond me, deeper into the tunnel. "Let's just get what we came for and get out of here. Your princess needs her elixir, and—" Fin seemed to catch himself. "And we wouldn't want to keep her waiting."

My eyes widened. As impossible as it seemed, I had momentarily forgotten about my mission—and my deception. In a weird and totally unexpected way, I was enjoying myself. I *liked* being around Fin.

Despite being appropriately wary of me—a relative stranger—Fin treated me with more openness and honesty than pretty much anyone I had ever met. I wasn't the princess to him. I was just some servant girl. And while he *was* using me, I didn't really mind because I was using him, too.

A seed of dread implanted in my belly. How would Fin react when he found out I was lying to him—and that Jake wasn't actually here? To be fair, it wasn't *really* my fault Fin believed Jake was being held in the prison; I hadn't exactly said those words. But I would have to come up with some way to distract him from realizing my ploy. Maybe play dumb when he figured out Jake wasn't here, then offer to sneak him onto the castle grounds.

I turned my back to Fin and chewed my lip as dread rooted deeper. The only problem with taking him to the castle was that Fin *would* try to free Jake, and he *would* get caught. And then he would be killed. I liked Fin. I didn't want him to die.

I sighed, my shoulders slumping, and continued up the passage.

The tunnel leveled out, and not long after, the pool of light cast by the electric torch touched a stair. Each step forward revealed more stairs until we were standing at the base of a long staircase that disappeared into the darkness above.

I stopped at the bottom step, and a moment later, Fin stood by my side.

"These stairs should lead to a common room in the barracks, in the northwest corner of the prison," I told him. "Only guards are allowed within. We'll need to find disguises if we want to move about unnoticed."

A thoughtful frown turned down the corners of Fin's mouth. "I don't suppose you know where the guards do their laundry?"

I shook my head. "But I *do* know the door to the tunnel is supposed to be guarded at all times. Maybe we can lure the guards down here and . . ." I held the electric torch in both hands and raised it high overhead, miming bashing someone over the head with it. "But not with this," I said, lowering the electric torch. "It would break."

"I've been pistol-whipped before, and it's definitely not fun," Fin thought aloud, and he rubbed the back of his head. My gaze drifted to the fading scratches on his temple and the slight bruise coloring his jaw. Ever so slowly, Fin's lips spread into a broad grin. "You know, that just might work. I like the way you think," he said. "I've got the perfect plan." He faced me, resting his hand on my shoulder. "Do you trust me?"

I narrowed my eyes at him. He kept asking me that, like we hadn't only known each other for a matter of hours and either of us had done much of anything to build trust. Yet, I really was starting to trust him. I had seen enough of his mind to know that while he would risk his own life to save Jake, he wouldn't risk mine, too. I nodded.

"Good," Fin said, squeezing my shoulder before letting go. "I'm going to hang back in the shadows. You huddle there"—he pointed to the place where the bottom stair met the wall—"on the floor. I'll pull back my nulling field so they can sense you . . . to lure them down here." He pressed his lips together, breathing in and out through his nose. "Maybe whimper or cry like you're hurt or something." He nodded to himself. "Once the guards are down here, distracted by poor, pathetic you, I'll sneak up behind them and knock them out. Then we can steal their uniforms, and we'll blend right in."

I chewed on my bottom lip. "I don't know," I said. "I feel like there's a lot that could go wrong with that plan."

Fin shrugged one shoulder and threw up his hands. "We could shoot them instead," he said, eyeing my bag. "But that'll be loud. Might give us away. Or do you have a better idea?"

I pursed my lips. No, I didn't have a better plan, and I really didn't want to kill the guards. It wasn't like they chose to be here; they were just following orders. "Here," I said, shrugging out of Fin's fur cloak and handing it to him. I fished the pistol out of my bag and handed that over, too.

Fin folded the cloak over his arm and took the pistol, nodding once.

Taking a deep breath, I turned and headed for the edge of the staircase. I sat on the bottom stair, curled my knees, then extinguished the electric torch and tucked it back into my satchel. I shivered and hugged my legs, closing my eyes as I dropped my mental guard. The darkness suddenly felt like a living, breathing thing, and I didn't want to be sitting here surrounded by the unknown for any longer than necessary.

There was a long stretch of silence during which my mind filled in the lack of sensory information with all manner of imagined things. Was Fin still there? Had he abandoned me? Did I just hear a rat scurrying down the tunnel? There was no sound beyond the thud of my heartbeat or the rasp of my breaths.

But then the unmistakable clang of a steel bolt releasing echoed all around me, followed by the creak of rarely used hinges and the scuff of boots on stone.

I held my breath and listened as the footsteps grew louder. Drew closer. The light from an electric torch appeared first, followed by a pair of guards—a man with a white circle around the raven's crest on his chest, and a woman with a red circle.

A male Telepath and a female Elemental. Elementals were extremely dangerous, regardless of whether they controlled water or fire, electricity or air. Almost any Elemental could kill with a thought by controlling their element within the body of their target. They could pull the water out of a body or the air from another's lungs. A touch could electrocute. Or burn. Fin had better be nulling them, or I was as good as dead.

Gritting my teeth, I hid my face between my knees and watched the guards descend the stairs out of the corner of my eye. I whimpered and sniffled, putting on a good show. If Fin wanted me to look pathetic, by the Patrons, I would look pathetic.

When the pool of light from the guards' electric torch reached me, the pair paused and exchanged a look. And then they hurried the rest of the way down the stairs. The Telepath crouched in front of me, while the Elemental stood guard, her back to me as she peered deeper into the tunnel.

I cursed silently. I needed the attention of *both* guards to be on me. Otherwise, Fin wouldn't be able to sneak up on them, and the whole plan would be shot.

The Telepath reached a hand toward my arm, and I saw my opening.

I drew in a lungful of air, then let it out in a shrill, shrieking cry. I kicked my legs and flailed my arms, and despite the Telepath's best efforts, I was too much for him to contain alone.

The Elemental turned toward me.

As soon as her back was to the tunnel, Fin rushed out of the darkness and bashed the butt of the pistol against the back of the Telepath's head.

The Telepath staggered. But he didn't drop.

The Elemental turned to assist the Telepath, her hands outstretched before her like she was trying to shoot flame or lightning at their attacker. At Fin.

I had no idea if Fin would still be able to concentrate on

nulling the guards while grappling with the Telepath as he was doing now, and I wasn't willing to wait and find out. I leapt onto the Elemental's back and wrapped my legs around her torso and my arm around her neck, locking her in a headlock. It seemed to take eons, but the lack of oxygen finally got to her, and she dropped to her knees, then keeled over backward, her body a dead weight on top of me.

With a grunt, I rolled the unconscious woman over and took a much-needed deep breath. By the time I sat up, Fin was crouching over the prone body of the Telepath, struggling to disrobe the man.

The Elemental wouldn't stay out for long; I could already sense her mind rousing. I skimmed her surface thoughts and memories, then stamped a quick illusion on her mind—when she woke, she would think she was safe in her bed, rousing from a strange dream, and hopefully, fall back asleep. We would have about ten minutes to get in and out of the prison before the illusion faded.

Finished with the Elemental, I crawled over to help Fin. Within a matter of minutes, both guards were stripped of their uniforms, wrists and ankles tied with bands of fabric torn from the bottoms of my too-long robe and gagged with more of the same, fresh illusions stamped onto both of their minds, and Fin and I were heading up the stairs toward the solid iron door and into the prison barracks. During my dip into the Elemental's mind, I had gleaned that the tunnel led into the small gathering hall at the center of the barracks and was currently empty, as it was the middle of the night.

When we reached the landing at the top of the long staircase, we tucked our bags, cloaks, and clothing into the corner where they would be hidden by the door when it was angled open. With a groan of metal on metal, Fin pulled the door open, and I slipped into the gathering hall ahead of him, my eyes scanning everything.

The gathering hall wasn't much to look at, merely a large, square room filled with long, utilitarian tables. The walls were dreary gray stone, and no windows offered a view of the outside world. The only decoration was a huge black banner displaying the silver crest of the Corvo dynasty hanging high on one wall.

Behind me, the heavy iron door clanged shut, followed by the snicking of Fin sliding the bolt into place. "Come on," he said, brushing past me and heading for the lone, open doorway leading out of the gathering hall.

The instant I lifted my foot to follow, the whispers started up again. I paused, just for a moment, then hurried to catch up with Fin. The doorway led to a long hallway, the brick walls on either side broken up by arched doors, all shut. Each one had a small view panel set into the door at roughly face height, covered by a steel slider.

"Do you know where to go?" Fin asked, pausing two steps into the hallway.

"Sort of," I said, stepping around him to lead the way. I cocked my head to the side and narrowed my eyes, letting the whispers lead me. It took me a moment to realize that Fin wasn't following me.

I glanced over my shoulder, and when I spotted him standing in front of the last door I'd passed, I turned and retraced my steps. "What are you doing?" I hissed, grabbing his arm and tugging him to follow. "We need to hurry!"

But Fin didn't budge. He tore his stare from the door, his eyes haunted. "Don't you hear that?"

I shook my head. "Hear what?" I couldn't hear much when I was focusing on the whispers, but I wasn't about to tell him that.

"Crying." Fin raised his hand and slid open the steel slider blocking the slit in the door. His eyes widened, and his lips parted in some combination of horror and shock.

"What is it?" I moved closer, my shoulder pressing against Fin's as I peered through the tiny window. Now that I was touching him, I could feel his emotions as if they were my own. His disgust twisted my gut, making me feel sick to my stomach. But it only took a moment for my own disgust to outweigh his.

The room was filled with eight beds, four in a neat line on either side, each occupied by a woman in a later stage of pregnancy. Each woman was restrained by her wrists and ankles, though none seemed to struggle. Their stares were glazed over, as though they were sedated—or they had long since given up. Only the woman two beds in on the right displayed anything beyond bored resignation. She wept softly, her chin tucked against her chest and her shoulders shaking with each quiet sob.

"What—what are they doing to them? Why are they tied up like that?" Fin asked. His voice was strained and he sounded like he might throw up. "*How* could someone do something like this?"

My hands balled into fists, and I backed away from the door. Hot tears streaked down my cheeks. "I don't know," I said, my voice hollow. I pressed my lips together, anger making my whole body tremble.

I had no idea why anyone would tie up a bunch of pregnant women like they were dangerous criminals. But I was determined to find out. And I was going to stop it. Mother had much to answer for, and I feared we'd yet to reach the worst of it. The whispers urged me on, and I had to follow. I had to know what was going on here. No matter how horrifying the truth was, I *had* to know.

Fin finally stepped away from the door and looked at me. His brow furrowed, and he reached for my arm. "Are you all right?"

I raised my eyes, meeting his. Rage burned through my blood, and my nostrils flared. "How?" I asked. "How could she do this?"

"The queen?" Fin shook his head. "Because she's a monster. They all are," he said, his voice edged with disdain. By *they*, he meant *me*, and I couldn't help but wonder if he was right. I had suspected Mother was up to something nefarious for a while now, but I hadn't done much of anything to stop her. Did my inaction make me just as responsible for what was going on here?

"Come on, let's keep moving," Fin said gravely, and I could tell he was trying to stay focused, even if he was just as infuriated and horrified as I was. "Where do we go to find your princess's elixir?"

I stared at him, confused. But then the gears in my mind clicked into place, and I recalled my lie. We were here to fetch healing elixir for the princess. "Oh, um . . ." I cleared my throat, once more focusing on the whispers. "This way."

I hurried toward the "T" at the end of the hallway and following the whispers, turned right, heading down another, almost identical hallway only some of the doors in this one were open. A lone guard rounded the corner at the end of the hallway, and Fin and I quickly ducked into the first open door on our left. It led to a stairwell that never seemed to end, which we hurried up, wanting to put some distance between ourselves and the guard.

The whispers were loudest as we reached the first landing. I stared at a closed door as the whispers intensified and pulled it open on well-oiled hinges. I nodded for Fin to pass through ahead of me, then followed, freezing after the first step. Fin was statue-still in front of me.

My gut knotted as I scanned the stretch of barred cell doors. Each prison cell was occupied by an emaciated man or woman wearing a simple gray tunic and trousers. There had to be at least a dozen cells, and this was only the second level.

I gulped, choking on a sickening combination of shock and horror. "Come on," I said, pushing past Fin and keeping my eyes straight ahead as I focused on the whispers. I hoped, desperately, that they were leading me to some answers.

The walkway led to a balcony overlooking an open common

area that looked to be shared by several cell blocks. I pressed onward, Fin close on my heels. Answers. This was all about finding some answers. Maybe once I knew what the hell was going on here, I would be able to do something about it.

When I reached the balcony at the end of the walkway, I gripped the railing, and the whispers stopped. I gasped, my blood going cold. This was what the whispers wanted me to see, and it was so much worse than I could have imagined. It was like I had been sucked into the resonance I had seen when I first touched the metal case holding the vials of healing elixir in the vault— only this was *real*.

The floor below was filled with dozens of stretchers, each holding a person, some struggling against their restraints, some passed out cold. IVs drained blood from their arms, and people wearing blood-red robes moved among the stretchers, changing out full blood bags for empties and depositing the full bags in a large, wheeled bin filled three-quarters of the way with ice.

This was it. The source of the elixir. *People*. In my gut, I knew what kind of people they were: Healers. The Healer Class wasn't dwindling. Oh no. It was alive and, well, not exactly *well*. But it was definitely alive.

I turned my back to the disturbing scene below while Fin still gaped down at the Healers being drained of their blood. I felt numb, unable to process what I was seeing. What it all meant. What Mother had done. No, what she was *doing*.

"Let's go," I hissed and started back down the walkway that had brought us to this nightmare. I'd seen what I came here to see, and we were running out of time to make a clean escape.

I could hear Fin's footsteps on the metal grate behind me. He followed wordlessly as I retraced our steps. Perfect. I wanted to get the hell out of this nightmarish place and get back to Castle Corvo, so I could confront Mother about the disgusting atrocities she was committing here. I hurried down the stairwell and headed back toward the hallway that led to the gathering hall.

As I rounded the corner, the gathering hall in sight, Fin grabbed my arm, halting my retreat. "What about the elixir?"

I spun partway to face him and shook my head. "No more elixir," I grated out. "This ends *now*." I clenched my jaw, daring him to disagree.

But he didn't. Instead, Fin nodded. "But . . . I can't leave yet. I have to find someone. He's—"

"Jake's not here," I told him, forgetting for a moment that I wasn't supposed to know anything about Jake or Fin's true reason for coming here. More than anything, I needed to be away from this place.

Fin released my arm and took a step back, his expression as stunned as if I had just slapped him. "What?"

I inhaled through my nose and met Fin's eyes. It was time to fess up. "He's being held in a tower . . . on castle grounds."

IO

FIN

"What?" I rasped as the passageway felt like it was closing in on me. My anger and disbelief at what I'd seen in this horrific place were eviscerated by a strange mixture of hope and dread. "Jake is at the castle?" If he wasn't here, it meant he wasn't a blood bank like the rest of them. But if he was at the castle, his fate might be far worse. I shoved my hands through my hair, grabbing hold as I stared Ada down, the possible scenarios Jake might be in booming to life.

"But you said—" I shook my head as I gritted my teeth. "Do you have any idea who he is—what they're likely doing to him right now?" My voice was sharp with fear. "They want his blood, Ada, *original* blood, and they're probably sucking it out of him right now, and we've wasted all of this time—"

"I'm sorry, okay? I needed to get inside the prison, and I knew you could help me. And now, we really need to get out of here." Ada's words fell from her lips in an impatient rush, and I frowned. There it was, finally, the truth. At least a partial one.

I'd seen the horror on her face earlier, so I knew she wasn't one of the royal family—she seemed too shocked by the torturous things they did in this place—but I was beginning to wonder if she wasn't really a lady-in-waiting either.

Had I been more daft than I thought, and this was all some sort of trap?

I took a step back, distrusting Ada more than ever. "Jake's not here and you don't really need the elixir," I said with disbelief. "Then why are we here, Ada?"

I watched her expression shift as closely as I could beneath the shadow of her hood; it was fierce in the flickering torchlight. "Why did you need to get inside this prison?"

Ada's brow furrowed, but I refused to believe it was remorse that settled over her features.

"Wait—" I whispered and straightened my shoulders. The distrust that had been niggling at me began to solidify in my stomach, and another wave of dread crashed over me. "You said *Jake's* not here." I shook my head and took another step back. "I didn't tell you I was here for him."

Ada chewed on the corner of her lip, blinked, and then opened her mouth to speak as footsteps echoed down the hallway.

"They're coming!" she said. "I thought you were nulling them?"

I was. Or, rather, I had been. My mind was a mess, and I hadn't been concentrating at all. I'd been too busy trying to understand what the hell was going on.

Grabbing my hand, Ada pulled me toward the gathering hall to hide, but a spindly, gray-haired guard stepped through the final doorway in the hall.

"You!" he said, pointing at us. His beady eyes narrowed. "Who are you? And what are you two doing in here?" I didn't know what he was capable of, and as I thought about Ada's pistol, I realized we'd left it back at the tunnel. I cursed myself and focused on the guard's mind. I could feel his Ability blaring like a bullhorn in my head.

The guard stepped closer, and as his Ability began to tingle in my mind, I took a deep breath and fortified my thoughts, nulling him again. *Null them all and find Jake.* It was all that mattered.

"Fin," Ada hissed, grabbing my attention. Her dark eyes flashed with warning as the footsteps we'd been running from in the hallway behind us continued closer. They were following our mind signatures too. "You have no idea what they're capable of," Ada said in a whispered rush. "We have to run!"

But it was too late. The other guard rounded a corner behind us, only this one was younger, with blond hair and broad shoulders. He was formidable, more so than the old man, at least physically. "How did you two get in here?"

Neither of us answered, but my mind and my fists would have to be enough to protect us now. Mentally, I reached for Blondie's consciousness. His mind was practically pulsing with raw energy—strong, Ability-honed energy—and with their Abilities primed and ready, it was a struggle to null both men; I could feel their consciousnesses fighting against mine, just as determined to overpower me as I was to overpower them. These men weren't just guards, they were sentinels, deadly ones.

But after years of training and stretching my mind—years of Jake's teachings, probably for moments just like this—my nulling shield amplified alongside my determination. The realization of what I was doing dawned on Blondie's face just as the old man stepped closer to Ada. I glanced at him and was met with a murderous gleam in his beady eyes. "You shouldn't have done that, boy," the old man warned with far too much anticipation. I could feel his Ability clawing at mine, squeezing it like a snake coiled around its prey.

I pushed against him, fortifying all that was left inside me, and groaned as my head began to ache.

"Stop!" Ada's voice resounded in the long hallway, and in an instant, she tore her hand from mine and stepped forward. "Stop!" she commanded again. Her hand flew to her hood and she tugged it away from her face. It fell around her neck, exposing her dark, braided hair and gold-brown eyes filled with a stout determination. Lifting her chin, she scowled at each of the guards. "Enough," she growled, and their death glares shrank to nothing. Their eyes turned to saucers, and they both took a fumbling step backward.

"Princess Delphinia!" The elder guard gasped as he knelt.

Blondie followed suit, but all I could do was stare at Ada, my face reddening, my mind whirling, and my mouth agape. *Princess?*

"Apologies, princess," the old man croaked. "We didn't know it was you. The queen never mentioned—had we known—"

"Nor would she, not when we've been assessing the defenses of the prison. It was the perfect test, and your guards have failed her, and all of Corvo City, for that matter. What if I'd been an enemy or spy?" The ring of authority oozed from Ada's voice, making my skin crawl. Not Ada—Princess Delphinia. The girl who'd helped me row all the way here—who'd been shivering, wet, and cold—now stood tall and confident, like . . . a princess. She stepped closer to the old man. "What is your name?"

"Uh—I am Merec, your highness." He dipped his head with awe and obedience.

"And you?" she asked, staring past me at Blondie, as if I wasn't standing beside her at all. "What is your name?"

"I am Rowan, your highness." Whatever threat I'd seen in him had completely dissolved as his hands clasped so tightly together his knuckles whitened. Fear and surprise made him a quaking fool.

"Well, Sir Merec," the princess said and glanced from one to the other. "Sir Rowan. I was told it was impossible to enter the prison, that the capabilities of my mother's most highly trained and noble knights were above reproach, and yet here we stand. The queen will not be pleased."

Sir Merec's head shot up and his eyes were wide with desperation. "But your highness—"

"How many of you are there?" the princess interrupted, and as she continued to berate them, all I could do was stare at her.

She'd tricked me. My hands balled into fists at my sides. Was that really why we'd come, to test the prison's defenses? I felt sick to my stomach all over again. I'd known she was lying to me, but this . . . the Corvo princess was standing beside me—a member of the most monstrous family, someone I'd been raised to both fear and loath.

I was shocked. Infuriated. Torn between hatred and awe.

"But," the princess said, her voice softening slightly. "As this is the first offense, missteps can be overlooked, as long as you make it your sole priority to remedy your shortcomings. You must train more," she said. "You must be more diligent from this moment forward. This cannot happen again. Do you understand?" The authority in her voice bewildered me.

Both men nodded, fear and relief shimmering in their eyes. "Yes, your highness," they said softly, and bile rose in my throat. The power the royal family held, and the terror they instilled in their people, was sickening.

"Good, now rise," she said and offered each man one of her hands. I was disgusted by how quickly they jumped to their feet and took her proffered hands in theirs, the way their lips brushed her knuckles with such reverie and utter obedience.

I watched as the princess's fingers squeezed around the guards' and her eyes closed. She pursed her lips, and her brow furrowed. What was she doing to the guards, feeding them thoughts? Searching their minds for answers?

"You touched me," I breathed, and as the realization trickled over me in cold dread, the princess dropped the guards' hands from hers, her shoulders slumping. What had she found in my mind?

The princess turned to me, weariness etching her features, and pressed her index finger to her lips to silence me.

When the men looked up, they had a distant look in their eyes, and without a word or even a rushed step, they filed up the hallway behind us and disappeared without another look back, as if they had never seen us at all.

The princess nodded toward the door that led back to the secret passageway we'd used to get in. But as she hurried toward it on light feet, my own wouldn't move. How many times had she touched me? How many memories had she already stolen from me, and what had she seen? More importantly, what had she changed, and what would happen next?

"Come on," she mouthed, jutting her chin toward the hall. I shook my head.

With a huff, the princess hurried back over to me, her dark gaze sharp and glaring. "Do you want to find Jake or not," she hissed. "Because he's not here, Fin."

My chest heaved as I stared into her eyes. Yes, I needed to get to Jake, but . . . would the Corvo princess, daughter to the queen who had ordered the capture of Jake at all costs—who had killed my friends and bullied and lied to her people—really help *me*? I nearly laughed with hysteria.

"I'm supposed to believe you?" I clenched my jaw, feeling my deep-seated ire burning in my cheeks as humiliation and disbelief branded me again.

"Believe what you want, but either way, you need to get out of here as much as I do. If Mother finds out I was here, it will ruin everything. You want me to take you to Jake, don't you?" She pointed in the direction of the guards. "If they hear us, it will shatter the illusion they're under. Is that a chance you want to take? They are some of the strongest Elementals we have, and even if you can null them now, you can't do it forever if they catch you, and trust me, that's the last thing you want. They can pull your insides out with a single thought if you let your guard down for even a second. It's what they're trained to do."

"Then why didn't you let them?" I bit out.

The princess looked surprised by my question, but whatever hurt I saw flicker in her eyes was quickly replaced with resolve. "Because despite what you think, I'm not a monster." Turning on her heel, she strode for the hallway.

Knowing I had little choice but to go back to the boat which was our only way off the island, I fell into step behind her, my feet moving automatically as my thoughts continued to grind together, misshapen and stilted.

Even if I didn't trust the princess, I believed she wouldn't hurt me. She could've given me to the guards and only saved herself. Or maybe I was just trying to convince myself she wouldn't hurt me, so I didn't feel so stupid for wanting to believe her.

The trek back to the passageway was a blur. My thoughts swirled, and I vaguely recalled the guards, still unconscious where we'd left them.

I'm not sure how much time passed as we rushed through the secret tunnel that would put us back at the boat. The squish of our hurried footsteps in the slick algae filled the air, and the breeze whining through the passage felt colder and more ominous than before.

If the princess knew where Jake was, did that mean she'd seen him? So many questions begged to be answered, but I didn't trust that her answers would be truths.

I eyed her closely as she walked ahead of me, her electric torch lighting the way toward the metal door.

As I fingered the fur cloak and the pack I'd reclaimed in the corridor, I thought about Beast. I missed him, his sixth sense and impeccable judge of character. He would know if the princess was being sneaky because Beast was the king of sneaky.

Bringing me here wasn't a test or a lure to bait me because

the princess clearly needed to get here so badly that she was willing to brainwash her minions in order to hide from her mother the fact that she'd been at the prison at all.

As the questions surmounted, I couldn't keep quiet any longer, even if the princess's answers were lies, I had to fill the silence. As we drew closer to the tunnel's entrance, I finally asked, "If you're the princess, why go through all of this trouble to sneak into the prison? And why bring me with you?"

"Because I'm not allowed here," she said hotly. "I thought that was obvious." She sounded far more annoyed with me than she had any right to be.

"Oh, I'm sorry, *princess*," I quipped, stopping behind her. "Are my questions annoying you?"

"Yes, actually, they are." She whirled around and stepped closer, the torchlight making her eyes glow like onyx jewels in the darkness. "We need to get back to the castle or all of this was for nothing." Her exasperation nearly matched mine, but I'd half trusted her once, I wasn't dumb enough to do it again.

"Unless you're lying, or planning to use me for something else." I shook my head. "You probably don't even know where Jake is."

"Oh, I know where he is," she said, her voice earnest. "I know exactly where he is because I've spoken to him."

I felt my face pale as I wondered what it meant that she'd been in the same room with him. What had she done to him? Or what had she *seen* done to him?

"Stop looking at me like that," she said, and there was a hint of regret in her voice. Or maybe it was sorrow. "I'm not like Mother. I can take you to him, but . . ." She shook her head like she knew the words that followed would be pointless, but she ventured to say them anyway. "But you have to trust me, Fin." The princess rubbed her temples, and for a flash of a moment I saw the shivering girl in the boat again, the one who was as determined as I was to get into the prison, now equally determined to get out.

"Look," she started, exhaling a deep breath. "I'm sorry, okay? Yes, I lied to you because I needed to get into this place and see what they were doing, and it was a lot easier to do with you helping me. I promised Jake I would find out what they want with him, and now I know."

A flare of hope swirled through me. "You mean, they haven't done anything to him yet?"

The princess crossed her arms over her chest. "Not that I know of. He's in a cell in the castle tower, and if we're going to help him, we have to get out of here before more Elementals come."

If Jake asked her to do this for him, that must have meant he trusted her, at least a little. With a renewed determination, I heaved out a breath, letting go of my reluctance, knowing I had no choice but to trust the princess. If she knew where Jake was, and *if* she was telling the truth, she'd spoken to him, and I desperately wanted to know what they'd said to one another.

"Why do you want to help him?" I asked as we continued toward the exit.

A faint sigh reached my ears. "I know you think we're all monsters," she said quietly, her voice small in the darkness and barely audible over the shuffle of our footsteps. "But that's not what I want to be. And until tonight, I had no idea Mother was so . . ."

"Evil?" I finished for her.

The princess reached for the metal door as if she hadn't heard me, and it squeaked as it swung open in the breeze. Then, she turned to me, her expression worried and her eyes imploring. "What is Jake to you?" she asked. "I've been trying to figure it out, but I—I can't."

Even though my brain told me to give her nothing more than she'd already stolen, I wanted the princess to know me. Maybe it would help her understand . . . maybe she really *would* help me. "He's the closest thing I have to a father," I admitted. I'd never said the words out loud before. "And he left me and all of his people behind to turn himself over to your mother—to save us."

The princess stared at me with an expression I couldn't discern, but instead of allowing her to ask another question or to continue thinking whatever thoughts crumpled her brow, I handed her my fur cloak and gestured toward the boat that was now floating in the high tide.

"After you, your highness."

With a glare, she stepped past me and climbed into the boat. "Call me Del," she said. "And that's not a request."

I tried to fight a grin as I untied the boat and jumped inside. "As you wish."

II

DEL

We rowed across the bay, our oars dipping, gliding, and reemerging from the surprisingly still water in a steady rhythm. The wind from earlier in the night had died down, and a dense fog had settled over the city, dissipating to a light mist over the bay. Our heavy breathing and the water splashing against the hull of the boat sounded impossibly loud, magnified by the stillness of the night.

Fin glanced over his shoulder at me as he rowed. "Say someone wanted to get into the city without going through the gates," he said, speaking the first words between us in the nearly twenty minutes since we set off from Prison Island. He returned to staring back the way we'd come. "How would they get in?"

I pulled my oars through the water and narrowed my eyes. "Why?" The single word came out as more of a grunt than a question.

"A friend of mine will be meeting us on our way to the castle," he said.

I paused rowing, my oars hovering over the shimmering gray surface of the water. "A friend?" I asked, breathless. "What friend?"

Fin chuckled. "Just a friend," he tossed over his shoulder, not looking back at me this time. "Come on, princess. Don't you trust me?"

I pressed my lips together, and my nostrils flared as I breathed in and out through my nose. I blew out a breath and continued rowing. At this point, what did I have to lose? "There's an old sewer main that was used to dump the city's waste beneath the western wall before the ancient system was repaired and we switched over to that," I told him. Part of me hoped he was deceiving me and intended to sneak an army into the city to destroy us. We were monsters, after all. We deserved it.

"We still keep the old tunnel open as a potential escape route," I continued, "should the city be attacked. The mouth of the cave is easy enough to find if you're walking along the beach looking for it, but it's monitored psychically, day and night."

Fin tilted his head thoughtfully. "Monitored for human minds, you mean?" he clarified.

I nodded, then realized he couldn't see me and cleared my throat. "Yeah. So I wouldn't recommend it to your friend unless they can shield themselves."

Fin was quiet for a long moment. "That won't be a problem."

I sighed, wondering what I was getting myself into, and continued. "Once your friend is in the city, they need to stick to the shadows and fog as they make their way to the castle walls. We'll meet them at the Great Raven monument near Corvo Boulevard."

Fin glanced at me over his shoulder again, flashing me a half smile that highlighted his dimple but didn't really reach his eyes. "Thanks," he said before returning all of his focus to the task at hand—rowing.

Soon enough, we reached the docks and were back to sneaking through the city. A quick check of my pendant watch told me it was half past three in the morning. In a couple of hours, the sky would begin to lighten, harkening dawn's approach. We needed to be inside Castle Corvo well before the sun rose, or I wouldn't beat the servants to my chambers and they would discover the artfully arranged pillows occupying my bed in lieu of me. Thankfully, the heavy fog masked our movements through the city. We kept our minds guarded, and with Fin's help, we easily avoided any patrolling guards.

An hour after disembarking the boat, we huddled in the mouth of an alleyway along Corvo Boulevard, scoping out the faint outline of the Great Raven. The behemoth statue carved out of black granite loomed over the divided avenue, its outstretched wings sheltering the empty lanes on either side of the grassy median. Spotlights made it glow through the sheltering fog.

I chewed on my lip. "I don't see anyone," I whispered. Any movement around the statue would have been obvious with the spotlights. "Where's your friend?"

"Sticking to the shadows," Fin murmured. "What's our next move?" He peered up at the night sky, not quite visible through the fog. "We're running out of time."

I scanned the area around the Great Raven. "Can you cause a distraction?" I asked, glancing at Fin. "Make some dogs howl down the lane or something? Anything to draw any watching eyes away from the monument for a minute."

Fin's eyes narrowed in thought, and he nodded slowly. His stare grew distant, and a moment later, a swarm of crows took flight, invisible through the fog, but their chorus of cawing was amplified by the heavy mist. Dogs soon responded with soulful howls, and the night was suddenly filled with an orchestra of animal sounds.

I reached for Fin but stopped myself short of touching his arm. "Come on," I said, voice urgent. "Let's go!"

Fin's eyes met mine, and he nodded.

I took off across the road at a dead sprint, pushing my exhausted body as hard as I ever had before. I could hear Fin behind me, close on my heel. When I reached the base of the monument, I raised my hand and pressed one huge talon on the left foot of the Great Raven into the base, waiting until it clicked, then did the same with two talons on the right foot. As soon as the third talon clicked into place, the sound of stone grinding on stone filled the night, and a squat opening appeared in the base of the monument, wider than it was tall.

Without hesitation, I dropped to my hands and knees and crawled into the passage. Once I was at least a dozen feet in, I paused and fished the electric torch out of my bag, then turned around to face Fin. And froze, my face mere inches from the whiskered snout of an enormous cougar.

My eyes opened wide, and I gulped.

The cougar chuffed.

"Um, Fin," I said, my voice shaky and too high. "Please tell me your friend is a giant cat and I'm not about to die . . ."

Fin's chuckle floated past the cougar. "Del, meet Beast," he said. "Beast, Del."

The cougar—Beast—stretched his neck out toward me, his whiskers tickling my skin as he sniffed my face. And then, without warning, he rubbed the side of his face against mine, almost like he was marking me.

"Hmm," Fin murmured. "He likes you." I couldn't help but notice the surprise in his voice.

I took a shaky breath, my eyes locked with Beast's. "Good," I said. "Great. That's great. Um . . ." I cleared my throat, trying to make my voice a little less high-pitched and shaky. "Fin, there should be a depression in the wall near the opening—about the size of your hand. If you push on it, the slab should slide back into place."

"Got it," Fin said. There was a scuffling sound as he presumably turned around to search the walls.

Tentatively, I raised a hand toward Beast's snout. I held my fingers in front of his nose, letting him get used to my scent.

The big cat's nose twitched, and then he rubbed his face

against my fingers.

My lips curved into a smile, and I scratched his scruffy jowls and along his neck. I could feel the solid muscle and sheer, coiled power hidden beneath his soft fur. A low rumble started in his chest, and I became very still, thinking he was growling at me. But the rumble continued with each inhale and exhale, and one glance at his eyes, narrowed to contented slits, told me he wasn't upset. He was *purring*. I giggled.

From behind Beast, Fin cleared his throat.

I craned my neck to peer past the cougar.

"We're sealed in," Fin said, his voice hushed. "Shall we?" He gestured down the tunnel.

"Oh." I lowered my hand and flashed Fin a quick smile. "Good," I said, and with one last glance at the deadly cat, turned my back to both of them and crawled deeper into the tunnel.

Another dozen feet and a staircase of brick appeared ahead of me. The ceiling height remained the same, but after the first few awkward, crouched steps, I descended the stairs and was able to straighten. As the stairs continued farther, the ceiling angled downward, the tunnel delving underground as it followed Corvo Boulevard toward the castle wall.

The tunnel exited through a hidden passage in the mausoleum of the first Corvo queen, and we snuck through the royal cemetery, hidden by the fog. When we reached the orchard, fruit trees loomed all around us, dark, menacing sentries. But then we were through, and the road encircling the castle moat was before us.

As we crouched between a couple of cypress trees, I peered up at the sky. Even through the fog, I could tell it was beginning to lighten. I scanned the bridge ahead, the only way into the castle. On such a foggy night, there would be extra sentries guarding the bridge. I could already hear their footsteps as they patrolled the length of it. We would never make it across.

I looked at Beast, then at Fin. "I hope Beast doesn't mind

water," I murmured, my voice hushed.

Fin's eyes narrowed as he glanced at me sidelong. "Why?" he whispered.

I offered him an apologetic smile. "Because we're going to have to swim under the bridge," I told him. "It's the only way we'll get to the castle undetected."

"He'll manage," Fin said with a quirk of a smile in Beast's direction. Fin held an arm out to the road. "After you."

I nodded once, then inhaled deeply, blowing the breath out in a slow, steady exhale. I moved carefully, placing my boots on the gravel road to make as little noise as possible. I eased down the embankment and made my way under the bridge, where I waited for Fin and Beast to join me.

Beast slipped into the water first, without making a single sound, save for maybe a hiss of breath. As Fin stashed his backpack and cloak in a crevasse between a couple of larger rocks, I removed my own cloak and double-checked my bag to make sure it was securely shut for the swim. Side by side, Fin and I eased into the moat, moving slowly as well, attempting to keep our breathing even despite the frigid water.

I swam with my head above the surface while Fin dove under, beating me to the shore. After Fin pulled himself out of the water, he held a hand out to help me climb onto the rocky embankment beside him.

I started to reach for his hand but paused, half-submerged in the moat. He didn't realize what he was doing, offering his hand to me like that. He couldn't realize.

Fin rolled his eyes and grabbed my hand, pulling me out of the water. Or maybe he did realize, but at the moment, he simply didn't care.

I shook off my shock and led Fin and Beast around to the far side of the island. We climbed up the slope, heading for a hidden side door used by the servants. Once we were inside the castle, we slipped into the warren of secret passages and snuck up to the hallway that led to my chambers, emerging once more from behind the painting of Dani, Patron of the Telepaths.

Fin's eyes took in everything—the painting, the lavish decor, the length and layout of the hallway.

I waved a hand and nodded toward the door to my chambers. Only once we were inside and I had eased the door shut behind us did I let my guard down. I leaned back against the door, shoulders sagging and breaths ragged, and closed my eyes. What a night.

When I opened my eyes again, Beast had settled near the dying embers in the fireplace, bathing himself. But it was Fin I watched, wandering around the sitting room, examining my knick-knacks and tilting his head to the side to read the spines of books. It felt extremely personal, the way he was studying these little pieces of my life. Pieces of me. Personal and intimate.

I cleared my throat and pushed off the door, heading for the bedroom. I was cold and filthy, and we wouldn't be able to do anything for a while yet, so I figured it was worth it to wash up.

Sid shifted on his stand, silently watching the newcomers with his beady eyes.

"Be nice," I told him as I passed by. I ducked into the washroom to run a bath, then returned to the sitting room and approached the window behind the breakfast table.

When I reached the window, the shadowy outline of the Tower of Solitude was just barely visible below, near the edge of the moat. I waited for Fin to finish his circuit around the room. He paused to carry on a silent conversation with Sid, then joined me at the window.

"That's where he is," I told Fin, pointing to the tower. I watched him out the corner of my eye. "But we're not going to be able to get him out of there. We'll have to watch from here and wait until they move him."

Fin looked at me, his eyes rounding in surprise. "We?"

I nodded, averting my gaze to the table and wrapping my

arms around my middle as a shiver racked my body. "I promised to help him." I looked up, my eyes locking with Fin's. "I intend to keep that promise."

Beast was suddenly on his feet, his tail swishing back and forth.

"Incoming!" Sid croaked, readjusting his wings.

My eyes widened in alarm.

"Someone's in the hallway," Fin said, his translation unnecessary. "They're heading this way."

It was probably just a servant coming to ready my rooms for the morning, but . . . "You need to hide!" I hissed, grabbing Fin's arm and dragging him into my bedroom, Beast trotting close behind.

I led them through the bedroom and into the washroom, heading for the door to the attached dressing room. Within, there were plenty of nooks and crannies where they could hide. I shut them in the dressing room and glanced down at my sopping wet clothes, then at the tub filling with steaming water in the center of the washroom. I stripped out of my soggy clothes as quickly as possible, hiding them in the hamper, and I was just about to step into the tub when I remembered the bed—I'd arranged pillows under the covers to look like me, asleep.

I raced into the bedroom and yanked the pillows out from under the covers, tossing them onto the bed. I could hear the door handle in the sitting room turning as I rushed back into the washroom, eased the door shut, and sank into the tub. Water sloshed over the edge, but I barely noticed. Only one person would ever risk entering my rooms without knocking: Mother.

Heart racing, I turned off the faucet and dunked my head under the water, then reemerged and sat back in the tub, closing my eyes and controlling my breathing as I tried to appear as relaxed as possible.

The washroom door creaked faintly as it opened.

I took a deep breath, willing myself to stay calm. "Hello,

Mother."

"You're up early," she said from the doorway.

I opened my eyes, gazing at her lazily. "Yes, well . . . I couldn't sleep."

Mother sighed. "It's a big day, I know," she said. "The welcoming feast."

I stiffened but forced my muscles to relax. My heart was suddenly pounding in fear for something entirely unrelated to the secrets I was hiding in my closet. Was the welcoming feast really today? How had I forgotten?

"You'll want to make a good first impression when you meet your suitors," Mother said, unaware of my inner panic.

I took a breath, inhaling and exhaling as evenly as possible. "Can't wait," I said, feigning indifference. I flashed Mother a tight smile and quickly turned my attention to the window on the far wall.

Again, she sighed. With slow, steady steps, she entered the bathroom, perching on a squat stool near the tub. "You know," she started, "I couldn't sleep the night before my welcoming feast either." She rested her forearms on her knees and leaned forward. "I stayed up all night planning my flight."

My attention snapped back to her. "You thought about running away?"

She laughed, the sound as musical as ever. "Of course I did," she said. "Here, these *men* were coming into my home to contend for my hand in marriage, like I was some sort of prize. As if I were a *thing*, not a person." She shook her head, her stare growing distant. "They were coming to take away my freedom. My future." Mother let out a bitter laugh. "I hated each and every one of them."

"But," she continued, as she let her memories flutter away, "then my mother reminded me why I had to do my duty. For the strength of the dynasty. For the strength of the kingdom. And for the people whose very lives depend on that strength."

12

FIN

I stood in Del's dark dressing room, wearing clothes still wet from the lake. Leaning forward, I strained to hear the queen's voice through the door.

"You'll want to make a good first impression when your suitors arrive." The queen continued, but my thoughts hung on a single word. *Suitors?* Now that I knew Del wasn't a servant to the princess, but that she was the princess herself, I realized that so much of the merchants and bustling outside was for her. And the suitors she'd spoken so bitterly about, the *strangers* coming to woo the princess, made the reality of what I'd learned in the past few hours even more jarring.

No wonder Del hadn't seemed happy about the celebration; she was about to be engaged to a stranger.

". . . my mother reminded me why I had to do my duty," the queen continued, but despite her pep talk, her voice was devoid of any motherly concern. "For the strength of the dynasty. For the strength of the kingdom. And for the people whose very lives depend on that strength."

I rolled my eyes. Was the queen seriously preaching to her

daughter about honor and duty? Did she even know the real meaning of those words?

Anger heated my chest, and all I could think was that she—the blood queen, as my village had coined her after learning what her rangers had done to their loved ones—was only a few yards from me. My coiled muscles hummed, and my heart hammered with the need for vengeance. I could end this here and now and let Beast tear her to pieces, then she could never command anyone to do anything horrible ever again. After all the blood she'd spilled, it only seemed appropriate.

But the thought shriveled as quickly as it had sprouted. No matter what hatred I bore the queen and the city she ruled so mercilessly, killing her would likely start a war my people could never win. Not to mention, another part of me couldn't do that to Del, even if I didn't completely trust her yet. She'd said she was going to help me, and . . . . I thought she truly meant it.

Beast's tail lashed against my leg as he waited impatiently for the queen to leave.

"You have a long day ahead of you," the queen continued, and I heard a rustle of clothing and footsteps on the other side of the door. "Think about what I said, and remember that all of this, no matter how great the cost, is for the greater good."

I glared through the door at her, biting my tongue and clenching my fists tighter. After a few bated breaths, the door shut again, and I waited for the all-clear.

Finally, Del sighed. "You can come out," she whispered. "But . . ."

My hand hovered on the door handle.

"I'm—I need a towel, please. Second shelf nearest the door."

Opening the door a smidgen to let the light in, I peered behind me at the rows of clothes both hanging and folded along the walls of the dressing room. The closet was larger than my entire cabin back home. It would look like a hovel to Del if she ever saw it. But the moment I thought the words, I regretted them.

Whatever Del was—spoiled princess, queen incumbent, heir to the Corvo dynasty that was built on fear and blood—she wasn't the princess I'd expected, and if she was telling the truth about helping Jake, then I dared to hold out a little bit of hope that she really was different.

"Fin . . . Did you guys fall asleep in there?"

"No," I said quietly. "I'm coming." I grabbed two towels from the shelf behind me—an additional one for her hair, like my sister preferred. I'd never felt cotton so soft. Everything in Del's life was the finest and softest luxury could provide.

I opened the dressing room door to a washroom bathed in the pale blue light of dawn. Eyes averted, I walked toward the tub and cleared my throat. "You'll want to make a good first impression when your suitors arrive, huh?" I said, repeating her mother's words as I held the towels out to her.

Del scoffed, and the water swished around her as she stood. "I couldn't care less what they think of me," she grumbled. Her fingers brushed against mine as she took the towels.

Pheromones. Beast could smell them wafting off me, and he made a mental note of it.

"Shut up," I muttered.

"What?" Del quipped behind me.

"Oh—um, nothing. Not you." I headed back out to the sitting room to wait for her and was met by the glaring black eyes of the raven sitting on his perch just outside the door. "So, a raven, huh?"

"Oh, Sid—yes," she said from inside the washroom. I could hear her scurrying around through the partially open door, rushing to dress. "He doesn't bite . . . hard," she added with far too much amusement.

I eyed the raven closely, opening my mind to his once more. *Loyalty. Protection. Love.* He was radiating with it. Sid ruffled his feathers in reply, not so much posturing as he was letting me know he wasn't sure how he felt about me.

I backed away to give him space so he could continue glaring at me from afar and walked over to the dwindling fire. Beast followed and plopped down in front of the hearth to continue bathing himself. For the first time in my life, I envied the sound and peered down at my wet clothes. The next few hours would be cold and uncomfortable, to say the least.

The washroom door opened and when Del stepped out, she was wearing a black cotton tunic and trousers, finished with leather padding on her arms and shoulders. Her hair was wet and impossibly black, and the long ringlets hung down around her shoulders.

She didn't spare me a glance as she strode through the sitting room, heading for the door we'd entered. "I'll be right back. Wait here," she commanded. She paused at the door and looked back at the raven. "Be nice, Sid," she said, repeating her command to him from earlier.

When she stepped into the hallway and closed the door, Beast and I looked at each other. "Don't ask me," I told him.

Crouching down, I put another log on the embers and watched the fire flicker to life again. Del had a hearth in her sitting room—I assumed in her bedchamber too—and her living quarters smelled of lavender and lemon. She had gilded mirrors, a plush red settee, and a library larger than any I'd ever seen.

I shook my head and let out a humorless laugh. Those were only some of the *many* glaring differences between us.

I walked to the bookshelves that lined an entire wall. So many different colored spines, each one containing a story or history or adventure I would probably never read in my life, while Del had probably read them all.

I liked reading. I devoured every book Jake and Autumn had ever given me, which was nothing compared to Del's collection. And yet somehow, I felt like I was the luckier one. Del could read hundreds and thousands of books, but had she ever left the walls of the city? Had she ever traveled anywhere or seen anything? Was this place a prison for her, like it was for so many others? Her mother's words, still replaying in my mind, made me think so. The queen had mentioned duty, the dynasty, and the kingdom. But what about Del?

The door opened suddenly, and Del stepped inside again, closing the door quickly behind her. "Here." She walked over to me and held out a bundle of fabric in her hand. "It's only a shirt, but it's all I could find."

I stared at it.

"Take it. It's a servant's tunic, but it's dry and less conspicuous than what you're wearing." She eyed me up and down. "You're welcome to use the bath, too, but I couldn't find any pants, so . . ."

"Uh, thanks. I'll just change my shirt." I draped the clean tunic over the red-cushioned ottoman beside the fire and tugged my damp shirt over my head, getting a good whiff of myself. It was probably a good thing Del had fetched me a clean shirt; otherwise, Jake's guards might smell me coming from a mile away.

I stood with my dirty tunic in my hand and looked at Del.

Her eyes flicked from my face to my chest, then met my eyes. If I wasn't mistaken, her cheeks were flushed.

After another awkward moment, I lifted the tunic higher. "Uh—what do you want me to do with this? I probably shouldn't just leave it here."

"Oh—" She took it from me and, holding it at arms-length, she hurried back into the washroom to discard it somewhere.

Beast blinked up at me. He smelled pheromones in the air again, only this time they weren't only coming from me. I grinned as I pulled the shirt over my head.

Kneeling back down to poke the fire, I tried and failed not to think about just how many suitors would arrive for Del, and if any of them were staying in the castle. They'd have their hands full, that much was certain. She was going to run circles around the poor bastards. My smile broadened at the thought.

"Now we need to find Jake," Del said, suddenly all business.

I glanced over my shoulder as she marched through the room, gathering her hair atop her head. She disappeared into her bedchamber, complete with a grand four-post bed. When she came out again, her hair was pinned up on her head with a stick, and she had a wad of clothes in her arms. "They moved him from his cell while my mother was here. He's in the castle, now."

I rose to my feet. "Jake's in the castle? How do you know that?"

She began tossing what looked like silk sleeping clothes onto the floor. "The whispers," she said.

"The whispers?"

Del blinked at me and waved my question away.

I frowned as I watched her grab her slippers from just inside the door of her bedroom and toss them haphazardly onto the floor, along with a belt and crimson tunic. "But before we go to him, we need to pack food and supplies for when we get him out," she said, assessing her mess. Hands on her hips, she nodded in satisfaction.

"Screw the food, princess," I said, taking a step closer. Del walked to her discarded satchel on the table and started unloading it. "Let's just get to Jake—"

"You don't understand," she said, whipping her head around to face me. "The castle, the grounds, and the city are all swarming with guards, especially now with so many outsiders flooding into the city. It won't be as easy to get out as it was for you to get in, and definitely not with Jake by your side." A guilt-ridden look flashed across her face. "And he'll need food, even if you don't. There's no saying if they've fed him at all while he's been here." Her eyes shifted over me again, assessing me this time. "Besides, when was the last time you ate something?"

I shrugged. I hadn't thought about food in a while. In fact, it was the absolute last thing on my mind, but I knew Del was right. What she didn't say was that we had no way of knowing what the queen or her guards had done to Jake since Del had last seen him. I thought of the poor souls in the prison, their blood being drained from their bodies as if they were nothing more than blood bags themselves. We didn't know if Jake would be conscious when we found him, let alone dehydrated, half-starved, or coherent for the journey home.

"Okay," I said, feeling my insides churn with apprehension as I processed all the unknowns. "Supplies, and then what?"

Del lifted a shoulder as she bit the side of her cheek. "We follow the whispers until we find him."

I still didn't understand what she meant by *whispers,* but I didn't bother questioning her about it. "And if Jake's with the queen? Or if he's surrounded by guards?"

It was one thing to be outside, where I could draw upon animal friendlies to help me scout and sense things, but here in the castle, Beast was just as much of an eyesore as I was. There was no sneaking around the castle for a hundred and forty-pound cat, much less a ginger, shaggy-haired woodland kid who looked distinctly out of place.

"We'll have to figure that out when we get to it," Del said regretfully. "For now, we take the hidden passages to the pantry and get some food and water for your trip home. Mother's an early riser, and now that she's awake, more of the servants will be waking to attend to her. Soon the final preparations for the welcoming feast will begin, and the castle will be swarming with people. We don't have much time."

I hated to be the pessimistic one who asked too many questions, but I was out of my element here inside the castle where, despite the enormity of the place, it felt claustrophobic. "Won't someone notice you're gone and come looking for you?"

"That's what this is for," she said and made a sweeping

gesture at the mess of clothes on the floor. "I made it look like I changed into my sparring clothes for an early morning session," she explained. "It will buy us a little more time, but if I don't leave a mess, they'll know something is off."

My eyebrows rose of their own accord. Del was a messy, rebel princess who could fight, think on her feet, wasn't afraid to get dirty, and heard *whispers*, whatever that meant. I was more and more intrigued by the second. "Clever."

Lifting the strap of her satchel over her head, Del draped it around her and walked over to Sid. He ruffled his feathers as he glared at her from his perch.

"Don't worry," she told him, a sudden pep in her voice that hadn't been there before. "I'm not leaving you behind again." She held out her arm, and Sid sidled up to her shoulder, his talons scraping against the leather guards on her clothes.

As the raven settled into place on her shoulder, he puffed up his breast, eyeing me closely.

I eyed him back. He was a protective bird, I'd give him that.

Del nodded toward the door. "Come on," she said and grabbed a woven bag from the hook by the door. She shoved it into her satchel.

"The coast is clear," I told her, knowing Beast sensed no one in the hall.

Slowly, Del opened the door and peeked out, and when she confirmed there was no one about, we hurried into an adjoining hallway.

The rising sun filtered through the tall arched windows, illuminating the portraits and maps decorating the brocade wallpaper.

My skin crawled as the likenesses of my ancestors stared down at me from the walls. Even if their likenesses weren't exact, that their images were hanging on the castle walls was unsettling. Did the queen truly believe she was doing what her Patrons would've wanted by draining innocent people's blood?

Or that the originals would condone her warping their beliefs—the teachings of my ancestors built upon endless sacrifices—into whatever the queen needed them to be to suit her purpose?

As before, Beast and I followed Del back into the narrow secret passageways by way of a portrait of Dani with her dog, Jack, and we were encased in darkness again. It smelled of must and was cool like the tunnels under the prison without the bright sun to warm the halls, but Del navigated the passageways expertly, even without her electric torch. "You use these a lot then?"

"Yes," she said absently as we passed a few doors that led to rooms and places I would never visit.

We passed holes in the walls that allowed pinpricks of light to filter in, and I glanced through a few as we walked by—peeking into meeting rooms and a couple of empty bedrooms. It was easy enough to guess that this was how the queen and her minions spied on her guests. How she learned their secrets and used them to bend everyone to her will when she wasn't plucking their thoughts from their minds herself.

After a few more minutes of walking in silence, the scents and sights of what Beast could detect filling my mind, Del turned a sharp corner and came to a stop. "The cellar is just ahead," she whispered. "Is it empty?"

Beast sensed no one. But he did smell food.

"It's empty," I told her.

Quietly, Del pushed the narrow door open and stepped down into a cellar. Beast and I halted behind her, eyeing the shelves of bread and sacks of grain, rows of ceramic jugs, and glass bottles. The scent of cured meat accosted me, and I could practically feel Beast's mouth watering. I peered up at the lobs of meat hanging from the rafters.

Del pulled the woven bag from her satchel, then grabbed a loaf of bread and shoved it into the bag. "Grab a few for Beast," she said, glancing up at the lamb shanks hanging above us. "But he better eat fast." She disappeared into an adjacent room, leaving us to our own devices.

Beast and I looked at each other, and he licked his lips. I reached up and untied a string of cured lamb shanks, then set it on the ground in front of him. The entire cellar reverberated with his instant purring.

Leaving Beast to his feast, I followed Del into the kitchen. She cut a chunk of cheese from the wheel on the counter and grabbed a piece of cloth from a basket that hung from a tether above her, then she looked at me.

"Have some," she said, glancing at the wheel of cheese. "It's Mother's favorite, so you know it's the best in the kingdom." I wasn't sure if it was disdain for her mother or just a wry state-ment, but I was having a difficult time understanding how different Del was from what I'd expected.

I cut a slice of cheese and licked my lips. "How is it," I started, and popped it into my mouth, "that you are so different from the woman who raised you—your own flesh and blood?" Jake wasn't my father by blood, but I still had pieces of him in all that I was.

"Who said she raised me?" Del muttered and wrapped the cheese chunk in the cloth. "There were plenty of servants to do that for her." She put the bundle into the bag with the loaf of bread and continued to buzz around the kitchen.

I cut off another cheese slice, feeling my stomach rumble with greed.

"How is it?" Del asked, glancing at me as she filled a deerskin with water from a barrel.

"It . . . tastes like cheese," I said with a swallow.

Del laughed and nodded toward the cellar. "Is he almost ready? We should go."

I silently called Beast into the kitchen and glanced around for a bowl to fill with water for him to drink. But Del beat me to it.

"He can use this one," she said with a smirk, and she reached for a large, well-used pot hanging above the giant gas stove and walked over to the water barrel. "It's Berta's favorite."

"Berta?"

"The head cook. And she's my least favorite of the kitchen staff."

"Really. Well, who *is* your favorite?" I asked, leaning against the counter. I cut another sliver of cheese.

"Lucian, the pastry chef. He lets me hang out with him and sample whatever pastries he's working on."

I smirked. "He sounds like a good friend to have."

"He is. Mother hates it, says too many sweets aren't good for me, but what's she going to do?" Del shrugged. "Berta, on the other hand, takes Mother's orders very seriously. And Berta hates Sid—says he's a vermin and too unclean to be in the kitchen—which makes me despise her even more."

Del set the half-full pot on the ground at her feet for Beast to drink from, and he began lapping up water happily.

"So," Del continued, turning to face me fully with a glint in her eyes. "Sometimes, when Sid and I sneak down here in the middle of the night, I have some of the chocolates Lucian keeps for me, and I fill this very pot, heat it on the stove for a moment, and then let Sid enjoy a lukewarm bath in it, you know, because he's so *unclean*."

The chuckle in my throat surprised me and I leaned my elbows on the counter, studying Del in the muted morning light. "And now the cougar drinks from it as well . . ." I toked and shook my head.

With a big, beautiful smile, Del shrugged. "I'm a rebel, what can I say?"

"Yeah, you are," I admitted, wondering how I could've been so wrong about her. "I like it."

Del's posture straightened and her easy smile wavered. I hadn't planned to voice the thought. I hadn't even known I was thinking it until the words were out there, too late to take back.

"So, we should probably find Jake," I said with a thick swallow.

"Yes. We should do that," Del answered in a rush.

I lifted the cloth wadded up beside the cheese wheel and laid it over the top as if we hadn't been there at all, then went over to the pot of water, where Beast was cleaning his muzzle with his paw. "Leave it," Del said as I reached for the pot.

When I looked at her, she was grinning. "She'll be so confused."

I chuckled again, knowing Del and I could definitely be friends in another life.

She nodded toward the cellar, and I followed her back into the labyrinth of passages. After Beast was inside with us, I closed the door behind him and turned, nearly running into Del; the food bag in her hand was all that was between us.

"The whispers were louder by my quarters," Del started quietly. "So, we'll head back that way and see where they lead."

I nodded, staring at the shadows of her face in the darkness. Even though I couldn't see her eyes, I could feel them on me, and fleetingly, I thought about everything I'd learned about Del in the hours I'd known her. Then I thought about all the things I didn't yet know but wanted to.

"Thank you, princess, for doing all of this." I felt my chest warm as I realized how much I really meant those words. It wasn't lost on me how bad off I would probably be without her help. I'd come into the city to scout things out with only determination and my Abilities to guide me. Now, I wasn't only close to getting Jake out of here, but Del had shown me more kindness than I'd ever imagined was possible from the princess of the Corvo dynasty. "This wasn't what I expected to find when I came here," I admitted. "*You* aren't what I expected."

Del licked her lips and shoved the food bag into my chest. "Don't worry about it. It's the least I can do," she said, and then she turned and headed back down the passageway, the same way we'd come.

As we continued down the narrow corridors and around a few corners, I told myself that whatever I was feeling for her was gratitude and surprise, nothing more. Del was the princess, after all, and after we found Jake, I would never see her again.

"Oh no," Del muttered, her voice hoarse with unease. She made a final veer to the right and stopped at a slender door with an ornate handle.

"He's in there!" I whispered harshly. Beast could smell him. "He's beyond the wall and he's alone."

Del peered back at me, disappointment—or maybe it was apprehension—in her eyes. "It's Mother's study," she explained. I didn't pretend to know what the significance of that was or to understand the emotions playing over Del's face. "Be prepared," she said so quietly I barely heard her.

"Be prepared for what?"

But Del didn't answer me as she heaved a deep breath and turned the handle. The door squeaked open, and I was almost too scared to look, uncertain what I would find, but once I stepped into the room, I couldn't look away.

A brightly colored mural of Del's Patrons covered every bit of exposed wall between the bookshelves and paintings that lined them. Dani and Zoe and Jason, Becca and Harper, even Jake himself—all of them were etched on the walls, carrying out daily tasks. Their likenesses were uncanny, and their images were big and vibrant as they looked down at us. Marble busts of them sat on shelves interspersed between books, and pages of writing were in cases situated throughout the room.

This wasn't a study, it was more like a shrine. And Jake sat in the center of it as he stared up at all of their lifelike faces.

"Jake," I said calmly. I could only imagine what thoughts filled his head as his past life surrounded him. But he didn't move or say a word. "Jake," I repeated, and Beast and I walked cautiously over to him.

Beast licked Jake's hand as I stepped around the chair to face him. His clothes were dirty, but otherwise, he seemed whole. He didn't look drained or depleted in any physical way. He wasn't even restrained. His jaw was hard-set as always and his five o'clock shadow a little more grown, but it was his eyes that stunned me. Their amber depths were dull and lifeless.

"Jake," I said more firmly this time. Under the encroaching fear, I didn't sound like Finlay the boy, but Fin, the man. "Look at me," I demanded.

But Jake stared straight ahead, completely oblivious, like he couldn't even hear me. He didn't move. He didn't even blink.

13

DEL

I paused just inside Mother's study, watching Fin approach Jake. I had thought—or at least I had *hoped*—the whispers might fall silent as soon as we found him, as Fin and Jake were reunited and their escape was within sight. But the whispers were louder than ever. So loud I had to fight the urge to cover my ears with my hands, not that it would do much good.

Fin whispered Jake's name, but Jake kept staring up at the mural of the Patrons, his expression empty, his eyes vacant. If it weren't for the steady rise and fall of Jake's chest, I might have thought he was dead.

"Look at me," Fin said, grasping Jake's shoulder and shaking him "Jake! Look at me!"

Dread was a leaden lump in my gut. According to the discussion I had overheard between Mother and Advisor Maylar, Mother wanted Jake, above all other Healers, for the purity of his blood, but also because she thought he might be able to lead her to more first-generation Healers. More people for her to imprison, damning them to life as blood slaves.

And I knew Mother too well to have to guess the rest. She had delved into Jake's mind in search of the answers he refused to give, but she'd prodded with such force that he had retreated deep within his own memories. Jake was lost within his own mind, a prisoner of his past. Fin wouldn't be able to wake him. *Nobody* would be able to wake him, save for another Empath. A specific kind of Empath. An Empath like *me*.

Hesitantly, I stepped forward, closing the distance between Fin and me. This wouldn't be easy. Resting my hand on Fin's tense shoulder, I closed my eyes and breathed through a shudder as his fear and desperation flooded me. It took seconds, eons, to get a grip on the sudden influx of feelings.

Opening my eyes, I cleared my throat and licked my lips. "Fin," I said, my voice tightened by the intensity of his emotions. When he didn't respond, I squeezed his shoulder and repeated his name, louder and with more force. "*Fin.*"

He tore his stare from Jake's face but remained crouched before the unresponsive man. His friend. His family. There was more love shared between these two than had ever been possible between Mother and me. The kingdom had always come first with Mother, and it would continue to come first until the day she died. Or until I did.

"What's wrong with him?" Fin asked, demanded. He swallowed roughly. "Why won't he respond?"

"Because he can't hear you," I said, sympathy softening my voice. "He's not here, not really." At Fin's incredulous look, I explained, "He's lost, deep within the labyrinth of his own mind."

Fin's expression darkened, and his rage poured into me through my touch, expounded by his hatred for Mother and everything she stood for. He blamed Mother for this—how could he not? Even he could surmise that this was her doing.

Overwhelmed by his animosity, I removed my hand from his shoulder, focusing on the floor and taking slow, deep breaths to calm myself. After one last deep breath, I returned my focus to Fin. "I can help Jake," I told Fin. "*We* can help him." I glanced over my shoulder at the study's main door. Mother wouldn't leave Jake unattended in here for long. "But we have to hurry," I added.

Fin clenched his jaw, his nostrils flaring. "What do we do?"

I held my breath, extending my open hand to Fin. "All you have to do is trust me," I said. "Let down all of your mental barriers, and whatever you do, *don't* let go." I gulped. We were about to dive into Jake's mind to hunt him down, and it wouldn't do anyone any good for both Jake *and* Fin to end up lost within Jake's memories. "We're only going to get one shot at this," I told him.

Fin narrowed his eyes at me. "One shot at what?" he asked, his voice laced with skepticism.

Shifting my focus to Jake, I studied his slack expression and vacant eyes. "At helping Jake escape from whatever memory he's trapped himself within," I finally said. I looked at Fin. He was staring at my hand.

An internal battle seemed to be waging within him. After a long moment, Fin's shoulders squared, and he placed his hand in mine, his fingers engulfing my hand. His palms were surprisingly rough, the callouses unyielding against my skin.

I stared at him for a moment longer. Fin trusted me. The proof was right here, in my hand. I blinked, stunned by the realization, and shifted my attention to Jake. With a deep breath, I raised my other hand, gently pressing my palm against Jake's temple.

And the world melted away around us.

14

FIN

The warmth of Del's hand was all that tethered me to where I stood as my thoughts swirled with foreign images and soul-stirring emotions. I could still feel the lingering presence of the queen's consciousness in Jake's mind, like seared burns festering on delicate skin. She'd been searching for answers, but she hadn't found them.

. . . She needed Jake, but more than that . . . she needed more people like him . . .

. . . She needed originals with pure, undiluted Healer blood.

But in her desperation to get answers from Jake's mind, the queen had poked and prodded too deeply. She'd stirred awake the most precious, protected part of Jake's mind, the place where he stored memories that were so raw, they were crippling.

Lives I'd never lived before flashed through my mind, each of them shredding parts of my soul, sucking my consciousness deeper into Jake's mind along with him.

Jake sat in a living room with Zoe nestled next to him on a couch, swaddling a newborn baby in her arms. But it wasn't only happiness in Jake's mind, there was longing too.

With shimmering, jewel-blue eyes, Zoe looked up at him. More real and striking than any painting or image I'd ever seen of her. "She has Harper's smirk," she said with a smile. "And Chris's nose."

"But whose Ability will she have—his prophecy, or will she be a mind healer, like her mother?"

Zoe's smile broadened. "If they're lucky, maybe both." But as Zoe said the words, her openness and ease faltered, and darkness shadowed her eyes. "Am I crazy for wanting this?" She whispered. "Even as terrifying as pregnancy is these days and how freaked out I get every time . . . I still want this." Zoe's cheeks reddened and her eyes clouded with tears. And as the love of his life yearned for a child of her own, Jake's heart broke for her.

He tightened his arms around Zoe's shoulders and pressed a kiss to her temple. "No, it's not weird," he said, forcing the same disappointment from his voice. "Things get more uncertain by the day. Soon, there might not be a safe place to raise a child . . . Maybe it's better this way."

Reluctantly, Zoe nodded against his chest, and Jake squeezed her tighter.

The memories swirled, and once again, Zoe's face came into view, only this time she had a baby belly and a mixture of fear and happiness in her eyes.

Then, everything changed again.

. . . Becca, the Patron of Oracles, was lying in a bed in a nondescript bunker, blood smeared on her face, Jake crouched at her bedside. "It would always come to pass," she rasped. "You have always known it. They will eradicate us all out of fear—all of you —" She took a ragged breath. "You must keep moving—you cannot stay. Do you understand?" Becca gritted out the words and gasped for breath.

Jake nodded as he took Becca's hand in his, Zoe lost to tears beside him.

Every beaten-up, exhausted part of Jake hardened with anger as he watched his sister take her final breath. Again. Twice he'd watched her die. Twice he'd failed her. And once again, they were running from power-hungry bastards who would never let them rest.

The Re-gens were gone—Becca was the last of them—and it was only a matter of time before the rest of his people suffered the same fate. Unless Jake could stop it.

Goose bumps rippled over my skin as a swirl of elation filled me, and the images shifted.

Jake stood with Zoe, her hair streaked with gray and hanging in long waves around her shoulders. In front of them was a couple standing in a field of green. An old man with an eyepatch stood before them.

"I think even Grayson has a tear in his eye," Zoe whispered, and she glanced at Jake. A lock of hair hung over a scar on her temple.

He squeezed her with a nod of contentment.

Grayson cleared the emotion from his throat. "And do you, Hope Anna Vaughn, take this man to be your husband . . ." His words trailed to nothing as Jake stared at his daughter, tall like her mother with long raven-black hair that curled down her back. An indescribable pride and heart-aching affection filled him. How was it possible there was still a man left in the world Jake believed was worthy of his only daughter, his and Zoe's little miracle?

"I wish," Zoe breathed, and she wrapped her arm around Jake's waist. "I wish Dad was here to see his granddaughter on the happiest day of her life." She peered up at him, eyes watery but bright with happiness, despite the pain she tried to hide from him.

The years had been harsh, and unlike Jake, whose body felt no effects of a lifetime of running and fighting, Zoe's did. She wore the years like badges of honor, wrinkles and scars alike, and he loved her all the more for it as he pushed the reality he knew would come sooner than he could bear from his mind.

In an attempt to stifle the impending heartache, Jake leaned in and kissed the scar on his wife's temple and rested his cheek against her head. "Your dad's here," he promised. "Both of your parents are." He saw Anna in the ever-present twinkle in Hope's teal eyes and Tom's crooked smile whenever she laughed.

I could feel the world slipping away from Jake, along with his control as a fleeting image of Zoe on her deathbed flashed into his mind.

Her face was deeply lined with age, her blue-green eyes weary. "You have to protect them," she said as he cradled her in his arms.

Silent tears streamed down his face as her voice caught in her throat. He tried to be strong for her, always, but everything inside him was breaking—his heart, his hope, his control.

"Promise me, Jake," she said with a gulp. "They're all we have left, our legacy. Promise me you'll keep them safe." Her voice was brittle and her eyes clouded with pain and sadness.

Jake leaned forward and kissed her lips to stifle his sob, his heart hammering in his chest as he swallowed an all-consuming sadness he knew would forever change him. "I will," he whispered. "I promise you. Always."

I felt Jake's anguish like it was alive inside me. Tearing at me. Pulling me under a rushing current of longing and fear and exhaustion until I couldn't breathe. I tore my hand from Del's hold.

"I can't," I choked out, shaking my head, and I took a faltering step away from them.

Del's eyes were wide and filled with tears, and I hadn't let go of her hand for more than a second when the study door cracked open, and the narrowed, beautifully etched scowl of the queen herself was staring back at us.

15

DEL

I sensed Fin was going to pull his hand from mine a moment before he broke contact, and I just barely managed to snap us both out of Jake's mind. I turned to Fin, intending to lay into him for pulling such a dangerous stunt—he could have been lost in there, just like Jake—but the handle on the study door started to turn.

The door swung open, revealing Mother, flanked by two knights. Thankfully, Garath wasn't one of them. I really didn't want him caught up in this mess.

Mother's eyes widened, and the three newcomers paused in the hallway beyond. They clearly hadn't sensed us, thanks to Fin, who was statue-still. Beast stalked out of the hidden passage, prowling protectively closer to us.

My stare locked with Mother's, and I pulled the dagger from the sheath in my right boot and held it flush against Jake's neck in front of me. A dribble of blood leaked from the cut made by the sharp blade, but he would heal. His body would always heal, even if his mind was broken.

Mother raised her hand, signaling for her guards to stand down.

Fin looked at me, his eyes burning a hole in the side of my face as Beast paced in front of us, a living, breathing wall of fangs and claws. It took everything in me to ignore Fin's stare.

Rage mixed with fear, making my breaths come faster. I could only see one way out of this. Mother cared about one thing more than she cared about her own life—her kingdom. Her legacy. In a twisted way, that meant she cared about me, most of all. I could use that against her.

I placed my hand on Jake's head, my palm flat against his forehead, and handed my dagger to Fin without taking my eyes off Mother. "If you come any closer," I said, "if you even move—I will scramble his brain and you'll never get what you're looking for."

Mother blanched. "Del, please, you don't understand—"

I scoffed, and a bitter, guttural laugh clawed up my throat. "Oh, I understand plenty, Mother," I seethed. My gaze flicked to Fin. "I'm going to be occupied for a minute," I told him. "Can you hold them off?"

Fin's eyes narrowed slightly. "What are you going to do?"

I looked at Jake, seated in front of us, his stare as empty as my respect for Mother. "I'm going to wake him up," I said. "And then we're going to get the hell out of here."

"Del," Mother said, her voice pleading. "Please, daughter—"

"Shut up!" I hissed. "Just *shut up*! You have lost every right you ever had of calling me that. I've been to Prison Island." I shook my head, my nostrils flaring. "The things you've done . . ." I spat on the floor to the side of Jake's chair. "You disgust me."

Mother flinched at the words.

I glanced at Fin, then at the guards. "If they move . . ."

He nodded, and his answering grin sent chills down my spine.

I flashed him a tight, closed-mouthed smile before kneeling on the floor in front of Jake. I reached up, clasping the fingers of both hands around either side of his head, a cage of flesh and bone, and stared into his vacant eyes. "Jake," I said, sending tendrils of myself into his mind, seeking out the part of him that was lucid. Aware. Lost. "Jake, wake up," I ordered, the tendrils still searching. "You have to wake up."

And then I found him, in that final memory, the one that had been too much for Fin. Too raw. I could hardly blame him. My cheeks were still wet with the tears born of Jake's complete and utter devastation. Zoe had been a clever one, her mind remaining sharp even as her body failed her. She had known Jake would need a purpose to keep on living. Something to keep his soul alive, even as his Ability kept his body going.

I closed my eyes and bowed my head, fresh tears breaking free. I hated what I was about to do to Jake. What I had to do to save him.

"Promise me, Jake," I said, my chin trembling as I repeated Zoe's final words. I wrapped those tendrils of myself around him, a lifeline pulling Jake out of his darkest moment. "They're all we have left, our legacy." My voice broke, along with my heart. I cleared my throat and pulled harder on the tendrils connecting us. "You have to keep them safe." As I said those last few words, I gave one final tug and opened my eyes.

A tear had formed in the corner of Jake's eye. He took a shuddering breath, and then his chest was shaking. Suddenly, a sob wracked his whole body, and he slumped forward, falling against me, dislodging Sid and sending the raven flapping toward a new perch.

I braced the toes of my boots against the rug and wrapped my arms around Jake, glaring at Mother over his shoulder as this strong, ancient man fell to pieces in my arms. "You will let them leave," I told her, my voice harsh but ringing with command. "And you will not hunt them or their people anymore."

Mother stared at me for a long moment. "Del—"

"You will do what I say, Mother," I spat, cutting her off, "or I will leave." I clenched my jaw, reining in the wild sorrow and anger raging through me until my voice was cold and even. "I will leave, and I will *never* come back, and your dynasty—your legacy—will die here, with you."

Mother inhaled and exhaled, her head held high and her shoulders pushed back, but I could see the fear in her eyes. The desperation. She would do almost anything to keep me here, to protect her legacy. After a long, tense moment, she nodded.

Tension eased from my body, but I didn't let it show. I tore my stare from Mother to focus on Jake, pushing him back gently so he was sitting up straight and I could see his face. His eyes were red-rimmed, but sobs no longer wracked his body, and his breaths were even, if a little shaky.

I slowly waved my hand back and forth in front of his face until I caught his attention, and his eyes focused on mine. My lips curved into a gentle smile, offering him what little comfort I could in such a terrible situation. "Can you stand?" I asked him.

He nodded, groaning as Fin reached out to help him to his feet. When Jake was finally standing, he leaned heavily on Fin. I could only imagine what physical torments they had unleashed upon him, a man who could heal almost any wound, to get him to spill his secrets. Torture—of a Patron—on Mother's orders. The knowledge made me physically ill.

I stepped out in front of our rag-tag party, and Sid launched from his perch on a bookshelf, soaring toward my shoulder. He landed and snapped his beak at Mother.

She narrowed her eyes, watching him closely.

Steps slow and even, I approached Mother, stopping in front of her and holding out my hand. "There's one thing I need to know," I told her, our gazes locked together. "Why do you do it? Why kidnap the Healers? Why breed them? Why harvest them?" I demanded. "They're people, Mother. *People.*"

Mother licked her lips. "I—"

"No," I snapped, thrusting my outstretched hand even closer to her. "Give me your hand so I know you're not feeding me more lies."

Ever so slowly, Mother extended her hand and placed it in mine.

I curled my fingers around hers, gripping them tightly.

"We're dying," Mother said, her voice little more than a whisper. "Our people are dying. Too much Class inbreeding has made us weak and sick, and the elixir is the only thing keeping this kingdom going." But beneath her words, I could see the ugly truth. Yes, many of our people were sick and would die without the elixir—but the affliction only affected the elite. Those who prized Class purity above all else. The vast majority of our people were just fine.

I narrowed my eyes at her. "You mean keeping the elite going," I said. "The *pure*. Without the elixir, all of your most powerful allies would die."

I caught a flash of her fear. Fear not just for her people, but fear for herself. She had been taking the elixir—not because she was suffering from some degenerative disease, but to stay strong and healthy when the burdens of ruling a crumbling kingdom threatened to crush her. Her youthful appearance was suddenly impossible not to notice.

Another, older worry trickled in from her mind to mine. She worried I was a carrier of the degenerative disease. She worried my children would need the elixir to survive, just as Calla, her firstborn had needed it. Only Calla had discovered Mother's secret years before I was born, and she had refused to continue to take the healing elixir. And she had died as a result, her death disguised as an assassination.

"The elite keep us strong," Mother said, steel seeping into her voice. "The elixir keeps us strong."

I shook my head. How could she be so blind? "No, it doesn't," I told her. "It makes us weak. Dependent. It turns us into monsters." I implored her with my eyes, pleading for her to understand. "What would the people say if they knew what you did to babies born with the healing gift? What would they say if they knew you stole and imprisoned their children—that you bred them and bled them? What would they say, Mother?"

Mother's shoulders slumped further with each question. With each word. She hung her head, her cheeks damp with tears. "It was for the greater good," she said, but the conviction had drained from her voice, leaving her sounding weak and uncertain.

"I know you believe that," I said, my voice softening. "You really do." I shook my head, fixing a hard stare on her. "But you're wrong." I was quiet for a moment, staring into her eyes, hating her for what she had done to our people. "We're leaving," I told her. "I'm going with them, but I'll come back. Someone has to fix the mess you've made." I squeezed Mother's hand tighter, digging deep for any hint of deception within her. "Will you try to stop us?"

Mother didn't even hesitate. She shook her head, and I could feel her submission through our joined hands. And I also felt it the moment some of the steel returned to her backbone. "No," she said, "I won't try to stop you." Her eyes met mine. "But if you don't return, Delphinia . . ."

I laughed under my breath, once again disgusted by the woman who had brought me into this world. If I didn't return, she would hunt down and slaughter every last one of Jake's people as punishment for my betrayal. "You'll never change, will you?" I said, more a statement than a question.

Mother held her head high, her stare hard. "How can I change if you abandon me?"

I held her stare, ensuring she had plenty of time to sense my intent. "I *will* return," I vowed. "But not for you." I released her hand and backed up a step. "I'll return for our people. Now, get out of our way."

Without another word, Mother moved off to the side and motioned for the two guards to do the same. Beast passed through the doorway first, followed by Fin, supporting Jake.

I remained behind, holding Mother's stare for a moment longer. And then I, too, left, and I didn't look back.

16

FIN

Standing at the bow of the sailboat as it soared through the water, I let the bay breeze, whipping over my face, divest me of the remaining mind-fog that Del's cerebral fingers had left behind—all of Jake's pain and agony, and all the memories I'd felt as if they were my own. I couldn't unsee them; I couldn't un-feel them, either.

I idly stroked Beast's head as he sat at my side, something I had been doing since we'd boarded the vessel Del had commandeered to take us home. She'd seemed as urgent to leave the city as the rest of us, and even if our village in the forest was only miles across the bay, it felt like we were traveling to an entirely different world, and I longed to be back in the comfort of the familiar. To see my sister, who was probably out of her mind with worry.

I glanced beyond the captain at Jake, sitting on the deck with his arms draped over his knees and his head resting against the wood-slatted hull. He looked better than when we'd found him in the queen's study, but not great. His neck wound was gone, but I wasn't sure his mind would ever be the same again.

Sleep. Beast's thoughts of Jake filled my mind, along with his concern.

Yes, Jake needed rest in order to regenerate properly, but I feared it would take a lot more than a good night of sleep to cure him this time. I'd felt his mind, and I knew how broken he was. He'd spent years pushing the past away, and now it felt as if all of it had happened only yesterday.

For the first time in my life, I realized that Jake's Ability was a lifelong curse, and I pitied him. It didn't matter how far he ran or for how many years he stayed hidden away and out of reach, Jake would never be free—not from his memories or his past, and not from the queen's reach, or the reach of anyone else like her.

The queen had let us go for now, but unlike Del, I wasn't convinced it was for good. I'd seen the desperation in the queen's eyes—the absolute need to appease Del, her sole heir—and people promised impossible things when they were desperate.

Side-stepping the captain, Del walked toward me. Her raven-black curls escaped from the knot on top of her head and whipped around her face, thwarting Sid as he gripped her shoulder against the breeze to stay upright.

Del was strong, and while I admired her for how she had stood up to her mother—the ruler of the Corvo kingdom—I didn't envy her for having to go back. In fact, my chest tightened at the thought.

Del stepped up beside me, shifting her worried gaze from Jake to me. "What happens now?" she asked, her voice almost a whisper against the wind. Sid ruffled his feathers and settled back into place on her shoulder.

"I take Jake home and let him sleep it off for a few days. And I pray my sister can help him in some way. Because without Jake to guide us, I have no idea what happens to our people next."

There was no going back to the way things used to be. I knew too much now, *felt* far too much, and I was determined not to live complacently, like before. And after seeing with my own two eyes what my people would be up against if the queen ever did come for us, we had preparations to make.

Del tucked a wayward wisp of hair behind her ear and looked at me, confused. "Your sister? What can she do to fix Jake?"

I dipped my chin. "Autumn's a healer—well, not in the way you think of them," I explained and pointed to my head. "She deals in herbs, but she has a way of soothing the mind." I thought about Chris and Harper from Jake's memory and wondered how similar to them we still were. "She can fix people sometimes if they open their minds to her—put them at ease a bit." After today, I worried Jake would be reticent to open his mind to anyone ever again.

I suddenly wondered if that was why my sister and Jake had grown close. When he'd returned years ago, battered and broken from one of his crusades, they'd connected in a way I'd never understood. Had Autumn helped him ease into his new life, and that was why they had a curious connection?

The love he and my sister shared wasn't the smoldering stuff Claire used to read in her romance novels. How could it ever be after knowing what life had once been for Jake, Zoe, and their family? But my sister's connection to him was there, none-theless; something strong and unspoken that I'd never compre-hended before. Is that why she was so patient with him, because she understood him like the rest of us never had?

My heart ached as I thought of Claire and the guys. It had only been a couple of days since my best friends' deaths, and now that I was returning home, I felt their absences keenly. They wouldn't be there to greet me when I returned to the village. We would never sit around the campfire again; Dallace putting on his practiced bard voice to read the most inappropriate parts of Claire's favourite love stories. I would never see her cheeks bloom as red as they had on those nights we teased her. And I would never hear my friends laughing again. *Ever.*

Reality would be so altered from when I'd left—the entire village would still be in mourning, and I would have to live with the horrors I'd seen in the city. Not to mention I was returning with Delphinia, the princess of evil in my people's eyes.

But what stung the most was that Del wouldn't stay forever, and when she left, I would have to mourn the loss of another friend.

"What's wrong?" she asked, studying me. Her expression was pinched with concern. When she stopped scratching Beast behind the ears, he peered up at her, expectant. "Is it your head?" Her eyes were wide with worry. Del rested her hand on my arm and pulled me to face her fully. "I told you not to let go in the study. I've never done anything like that before. I could've—"

"I'm fine," I told her, trying not to smile at how cute she was when she was concerned. Even if she was still ornery. "It's just . . . the last few days have been a lot, you know? What the rangers did to my friends, what you and I saw in the prison, and with Jake—all of it. How do we come back from all of that?"

Del blinked, and a few seconds passed before she pursed her lips and slowly shook her head. "I don't know," she admitted, and her words vanished with the wind. "I really don't know."

We stood in silence again, staring out at the wooded ridgeline as the horizon drew closer. My entire world had been turned upside down in the span of a few days, and I hated to think what the next twenty-four hours would bring. More chaos and confusion? More heartache?

I looked at Del, wondering what thoughts churned behind her dark eyes. "Why did you decide to come back with us?" I asked. It wasn't that I didn't want her to, but for some reason, her answer mattered to me, probably more than it should.

Del's gaze shifted from me to the cliffs and jutting redwoods we sailed toward. "Curiosity," she admitted. "And your people deserve an apology for what's happened, even if I know it fixes nothing." Suddenly her brow furrowed and her gaze shot to mine, less certain. "Do you think that's a bad idea?"

Del glanced at Jake behind us, as if she were tallying all the ways and reasons this could go terribly wrong.

I shrugged. I wished I could tell her that everyone would warm to her eventually, despite her name and lineage, especially once they knew her the way I did. But I had a feeling Del wouldn't be sticking around long enough for that. My heart sank with an unexpected heaviness. "You didn't mention *when* you'd be returning to the city," I realized aloud.

Del chewed on her bottom lip, her eyes thoughtfully fixed on mine. "I'm not sure," she finally admitted. I couldn't tell if there was an underlying question in her answer, or if it was a simple fact.

"There's no rush, you know? You could stay a while." I couldn't help the smirk that tugged at the corner of my mouth. "It wouldn't hurt your mother to stew for a bit."

Del rolled her eyes, more exasperated and exhausted than anything, but she smiled, just a little. "I wish it was that easy."

"Do you?" The words fell from my lips, more earnest than I'd expected. What *did* Del want? Now that she knew what the queen was capable of, and about our lives out here, what was it that she longed for—a gilded cage or freedom, with me?

"Do I *what*?"

"Do you wish it was that easy?" I urged, feeling a sudden flourish of nerves. "Do you *want* to stay?" For some reason, I couldn't bring myself to ask her outright, but by Del's response, I didn't have to. Her cheeks blushed and her eyebrows rose ever so slightly.

But as Del's brow furrowed and her silence hung between us, I realized how dumb my question had been.

"Actually," I said, forcing another smirk, "scratch that." I rested my elbows on the railing. "It's too boring out here, and I know how much you like your adventures."

Del frowned. "Fin, I—"

"Your Highness!" the captain called against the wind.

Del's posture instantly straightened and her princess-face slipped into place as we both turned to him.

"We're about a mile out!" he called. "Where would you like me to drop anchor?"

Del's eyes flashed to mine, and I couldn't tell if she was regretful or relieved for the interruption. "I think we both know you're the seafarer of the two of us." With an exaggerated gesture toward the captain, Del flashed me a crooked grin. "If you'd be so kind as to direct him . . ."

"As you wish, princess."

17

DEL

I lowered the oar into the water and heaved in time with Fin. Over and over again. We rowed the small boat ever closer to shore, the sailboat silhouetted behind us by the setting sun and gleaming water. Jake sat on the bench near the stern of the rowboat, his stare distant—though thankfully not vacant, like before. He was lost in thought, but not lost within his own mind. Beast lay sprawled out between Jake's feet and ours, and Sid soared overhead, coasting on the bay breeze.

"Just . . . a few . . . more . . ." Fin grunted as we rowed. "Alright, raise your oar," he said, pulling his into the boat and twisting around on the bench we shared. He stood carefully and stepped over the bench to stand crouched in the bow.

I turned to watch as we glided into shore. The sandy beach stretched out in either direction, and a steep cliffside jutted out of the sand farther in. A waterfall poured over the top of the cliff, the freshwater streaming down the beach and into the sea. I stared in wonder. I had never seen anything like this before—I'd barely ever left the city walls—and I almost couldn't believe my eyes. This place was so foreign. So wild. So *other*.

I had been so certain about coming here, but now that we

were actually here, nerves twisted my stomach into knots. These people would never accept me. I had seen in Fin's mind all Mother had put them through—all the suffering at the hands of her rangers. All the death and sorrow. It had taken a lot for Fin to see past his hatred of the kingdom and to really *see* me. I had earned his trust through action—I had proven myself to him—but how could I do the same with the rest of his people. All I had now were words, and I feared words would do little to wear down their well-honed animosity.

Fin leapt onto the sandy beach just as the hull scraped the bottom. He immediately turned to grip the bow of the boat with both hands, waiting for Beast to follow him before pulling the boat farther ashore.

"Jake," I murmured. When he looked at me, I nodded toward the beach. "Ready to go?"

Jake blinked, looking around like he was just realizing where we were. Home, or as close as anything ever would be to him without *her*. He stood and took slow, unsteady footsteps toward the bow. Fin helped him out of the boat and onto shore, and once Fin released his hand, Jake wandered closer to the falls and sat on a dry patch of rock. The centuries of life seemed to weigh down heavier on the ancient Healer now, weakening him from within.

I tossed Fin the line, then gripped his offered hand and hopped out onto the beach. "So, I've been thinking—could you maybe *not* tell your people who I am?" I asked, avoiding eye contact as we hauled the empty boat higher up on the shore, beyond the reach of the changing tide. "At least, not until after I'm gone?" I raised my eyes to meet Fin's.

His gaze was searching, and for a long moment, he didn't say anything. "This is good enough," he muttered as he tied the rope around a large oblong stone angled toward the waterfall. When Fin was finished, he straightened and stared out at the sea, pondering my request. "And when will you be gone?"

"I'll leave in the morning," I told him. "First thing." I knew he wanted me to stay longer. I had sensed it during the trip here. It wasn't that I didn't want to stay for a while, but to do so would put Fin and Jake at risk. It would endanger all of their people, and I just couldn't do it. "The longer I'm gone," I told him, "the more likely it is that Mother will decide I've fled and send the might of the kingdom after you. If you thought it was bad before . . ." I shook my head, willing him to understand.

Fin blew out a breath, his attention drifting to Jake, still perched on that rock watching the sun sink into the sea. "Yeah," Fin said, "sure. Your secret's safe with me." He laughed under his breath, though there was no humor in the sound. "And I don't think *he'll* be telling anyone much of anything any time soon."

I nodded, placing a hand on Fin's arm. "He *will* be fine . . . eventually," I assured him. "Or, whatever passes for fine for him."

Fin grunted, then heaved a sigh. "I really hope you're right. I know it's selfish to want to keep him here." And I knew Fin didn't mean *keep him here*, as in *this place*, but here, as in *alive*. "But we still need him. *I* still need him."

"One day," I said, "you'll have to let him go."

Fin stared at the man who was like a father to him. "But not yet," he said, looking at me, his eyes filled with uncertainty.

I shook my head, a sad smile curving my lips. "No, not yet."

We headed toward the falls and retrieved Jake, and soon enough, we were climbing up a path cut into the face of the cliff in such a way that it was almost completely hidden from the shore. Beast took the lead, followed by Fin and Jake, with me bringing up the rear. Sid was hunting, and Fin had let him know to return to the sailboat rather than join us ashore, for the sake of concealing my identity.

The trail atop the cliff was narrow and winding, and the forest surrounding us was surprisingly dense, dimming the already fading light. I wondered if someone in the village had some control over the foliage, allowing these people to encourage the forest to conceal them better. I had never met anyone with the talent, but I had heard rumors. Some rumors were just that, but some were based in truth.

We had just passed a fork in the trail and the way ahead broadened when a slight, blonde woman rounded a curve in the trail ahead. Her expression was wild and hopeful, and her long curls streamed behind her as she ran toward us, making her appear like an ethereal fairy creature in the twilit forest.

"You're back!" she exclaimed breathlessly, slowing to a walk. "Oh, thank God! I thought I would never see you again." She stopped in front of Fin and Jake, and as she scanned the latter, her keen stare seemed to note each and every one of his partially healed injuries. Her eyes lingered on his face, on his dazed stare, before shifting to Fin. "But you came back," she said. "And you found him—and none too soon, from the looks of it." Her chin trembled. "I was so scared, little brother." She threw her arms around Fin, though he was anything but little compared to her, squeezing her eyes shut and holding him tight.

I was overcome by awkwardness. This was a private moment, and I didn't belong here. I took a step backward, then another, second-guessing my decision to come.

"I thought I made a mistake telling you to go after him," she said, her voice thick with emotion. "I thought you were dead and—"

"Hey, hey," Fin said, rubbing her back as she sobbed silently against his shoulder. "It's all right, Autumn. I'm all right."

Autumn took a deep, shaky breath and pulled away from her brother, wiping away her tears with quick swipes of her fingers. "So, what happened?" she said, sniffling. "I want to hear everything." Her focus shifted past Fin, finally landing on me, and her expression clouded with uncertainty. "And who is this?"

Fin turned partway, holding his arm out to me. "This is Del," he said, taking a step my way. "She helped me get Jake out of there. I couldn't have done it without her." Fin laughed and shook his head. "I owe her my life—mine and Jake's both."

Autumn's eyebrows rose, and she regarded me with renewed interest. "Well then," she said, a warm smile transforming her face, "I owe you my gratitude. You are welcome in our village and our home for as long as you would like to stay." Her focus flitted from me to Fin and back, like she was wondering if there was more between us.

I blushed, despite not knowing why. "Just for the night," I told her, "and then I'll be out of your hair."

Autumn's smile wavered. "Well, if you change your mind, the offer still stands." She nodded to me then moved closer to Jake, pulling his arm over her shoulders and curling hers around his waist, more for comfort than support. "Come on, big guy," she murmured. "Let's get you inside and cleaned up."

She headed back the way she had come, and Fin, Beast, and I followed.

I almost missed the first few cabins, they blended in so well with the forest, almost looking like they had grown there rather than been built. But within a matter of minutes, we were in the heart of their village, and the cabins, as remarkable as they were, faded into the background as the people captured my attention. Some moved about, others sat on porches or within shelters, working on what I assumed were daily tasks.

A young girl spread seed to chickens inside a pen while a little boy whittled a long stick on a stool beside her. An old woman hummed to herself as she molded clay in her hand, a bowl beginning to form. A man hung meat in a hut, doing a double take as he watched us pass. Regardless of what the villagers were doing, they exuded a sense of purpose. Of peace and contentment.

I came here looking for proof that there really was another way—a better way—to live. To thrive. And yet, I found myself scanning the people's faces for hints of dissatisfaction or even fear. For the things I was so used to seeing on the faces of those living in Corvo City. But everyone here seemed at ease, content with their existence in a way that was entirely foreign to me. I hadn't known people could live so peacefully, and I could practically feel their calm seeping into me.

All the struggles in Corvo City seemed centered around the Class system and our yearning for purity. But now I could see that the thing that formed the very basis of our society was a construct, if not created by those in charge—like Mother—at least used by them to their advantage. We were destroying ourselves in our attempt to achieve something that didn't matter. Something that wasn't real: purity.

We entered a clearing that seemed like a wooded town square. Some people were already gathered there, while others trickled in from various paths. Autumn and Jake followed one of those paths, disappearing into a cozy-looking cabin.

Fin's people greeted him, congratulating him on his victorious return, relieved he'd come back to them in one piece. A few young women eyed me warily, mistrust written all over their faces. Not because they suspected who I was, but because they worried about *what* I was to Fin. Everyone else, however, greeted me warmly, if a little shocked to have a visitor.

A bonfire was built, and food and ale were brought out as people gathered to hear Fin regale his daring journey.

I moved off to the side, sitting on an upturned stump that had been set near the fire, listening as he recounted our adventures, thankfully glossing over the details that would have revealed my true identity. And I assumed it was also watered down to spare them some of the more horrible truths, at least for now.

He offered them versions of the truth and recounted the types of merchants he saw, the shops and the smells of Corvo City, in a way that held the villagers' attention. He made them cringe and laugh, and others cheered to his safe return over and over until they forgot the horrific reason he'd left to begin with.

By the time he finished, I was staring into the dancing flames. It seemed almost impossible so much had happened in so little time. In just a matter of days, everything had changed.

"What's on your mind?" Fin asked as he scooted a stump closer to my perch and sat, his shoulder brushing mine. He handed me a cup of wine and tapped his own cup against mine before taking a swig.

I sipped the wine and eyed him. "You know, I haven't heard the whispers since we left the castle," I said. I had told him all about the whispers on the trip over. He knew as much as I did now—which wasn't really saying much. They had been born of a resonance centered around Mother and Zoe's book, and like voices from the distant past, the whispers had guided me toward a specific end. "I think this is what they wanted—for me to help you guys, then to come here and see this. To see how much better we could be."

"You could stay," Fin said, not for the first time. "Have you considered that's what they want? That you don't have to go back there and be married off to the highest bidder?" I was surprised by his intensity as he spoke. "We can hide you from her along with the rest of us, just like we've always done."

I stared into the flames and let myself imagine, just for a moment, what life might be like for me here. What a life with Fin might be like. I leaned my head on his shoulder and smiled to myself. It was a pretty fantasy. An impossible one, but pretty, nonetheless.

"Nobody ever needs to know who you really are," Fin added, his arm curling around my shoulders. "Don't you deserve the chance to have a life of your own? To choose your own path?"

But he couldn't see that that was exactly what I was doing. It might not have been the path I wanted, but it was the path that needed me most. "I can't," I told him in a dreamy tone. I had already had several generous cups of wine, and it was starting to show. "You know I can't." I sighed, then yawned and closed my eyes.

"I know," he said softly. "But it was worth another try." Fin's body was warm and protective beside me, and my mind began to float away.

I woke to the sensation of something wet soaking through my pant leg over my knee. I had drifted off and spilled my wine.

"All right," Fin said, "let's get you inside. It's been a long couple of days. Even princesses have to rest at some point."

"Shhh . . ." I straightened and looked around, making sure nobody could have overheard.

Fin smirked and held a hand out to me as he stood. "Come on, tough stuff."

I took his hand and let him pull me to my feet. He led me out of the clearing and along a winding trail uphill. I was about to ask him if we were lost when a cabin came into view, and I noticed Beast lounging on the porch in a patch of moonlight.

"Hello, sweet Beasty," I cooed, smiling down at him, and he flicked his tail and yawned in answer. "You and me both," I said through a yawn of my own.

Fin opened the door to the cabin and led me inside. The soft scent of earth and leather hit my nose. The interior was small and bathed in shadows and streams of moonlight, and in no time, Fin had me settled on a couch in the main room with a couple of pillows propping up my head and a handmade quilt tucked around me.

Fin brushed a loose curl out of my face, gently tucking it behind my ear. "Get some rest, Del," he whispered, turning away from the couch.

I reached for his hand and gave it a squeeze. "Thanks, Fin."

He turned back to me, his brow furrowed. "For what?"

I smiled sleepily. "For everything."

With a flush of his cheeks, he ducked his head and rubbed

the back of his neck. Then, releasing my hand, he retreated into his bedroom, leaving the door cracked open an inch or two. It was just enough for me to watch him tug his shirt over his head in the dim light of a lantern before he stepped out of sight.

My heart was suddenly pounding in my chest, and I couldn't tear my eyes away from the crack in the door.

This was it—what Hills had been talking about. This was my chance to have something just for me. My chance to create a memory that I could hold on to through all the hard times that lie ahead. My chance to experience the life I could have had, had I been anyone else, if only for a night. My chance to have Fin.

I sat up, then stood and padded to the bedroom door. The door creaked as I pushed it open, and Fin straightened from a washbasin in the corner, water dripping down his face to his bare chest. His physique was lean but strong, his muscles well defined beneath the smattering of tawny chest hair.

His eyes met mine, surprise giving way to understanding. To desire.

Taking a deep breath, I stepped into the bedroom and shut the door.

EPILOGUE
FIN

ONE MONTH LATER

"*My people need me, Fin, you know that. Just like you said your people need you.*" *Del's brown eyes were wide, full of hope and determination. As much as I admired her for it, I greedily wished she wasn't so noble. "Think of all we can change."*

I snorted. "I keep my people safe and free, and you change a kingdom? Seems easy enough."

She rolled her eyes and pushed my shoulder playfully. "I'm serious, Fin—"

I grabbed Del's hand, holding it against my chest, trying to imagine a future in which our paths would cross again and under much more pleasant circumstances: the future Del saw. The one we both wanted to work toward, even if it felt like we'd been dealt the shittiest hand in the process. "I know you are, princess." I tucked a dark ringlet behind her ear. "Now that you know what your moth-

er's been grooming you for, what happens this weekend at the Bicentennial Celebration?"

She looked at me askance. "You mean, will I still announce an engagement?"

Clenching my jaw, I nodded reluctantly.

Del studied me thoughtfully, and I began to squirm under her gaze. "Everything is different now," she finally said. "Mother knows that. I don't know exactly what my future looks like, other than that I'm going to release the Healers from the prison, but I know there's too much I still don't understand before I make any hasty decisions." Her gaze scoured my face, and the longer we stared at one another, drinking each other in, the more the blush on her cheeks deepened. I'd never met anyone like her, nor was I likely to ever again.

Finally, she licked her lips. "I should go."

"I know," I said, hoping her answer meant she wasn't jumping into an engagement, at least. Heaving out a breath, I took a step away. "Your ship awaits, my lady." I gestured toward the rowboat that would take her to the sailboat anchored offshore.

Taking Del's hand, I helped her climb into the rowboat. "The waters are choppy today, tough stuff, so be careful and show those oars who's boss."

"I will," she said with a chuckle, and she flashed me a smile over her shoulder. Before she let go, she squeezed my hand in hers. "Goodbye, Fin."

I dipped my chin in answer, not wanting to repeat the words for fear they would be true, and I pushed the rowboat into the sea. "Safe travels, princess."

Our eyes met one last time as Del took the oars in hand. It seemed like a cruel joke that the first time I'd met her, we'd been rowing toward something together, and now she was rowing away from me.

For now.

"Hey, princess!" I called as the boat sloshed farther out to sea.

Del cupped her hand over her eyes to see me in the bright morning light.

"This isn't goodbye, you know. You haven't gotten rid of me that easily."

The corner of her mouth quirked with a barely-there smile. "Don't I know it," she retorted.

I'd stood on that shore until the sailboat's tall mast was no more than a pinprick on the horizon, and our farewells had filled my mind every moment since.

I shoved my bedroll into my pack with the rest of my things for my trek north, and I donned my long sleeves for the gusty weather along the coast.

Del was right about us. Nothing was the same now; we had futures to embrace that would change the fate of both of our people, and it was only possible if we did it together, just not the way we necessarily wanted.

After rescuing Jake from the queen and learning the awful truth about what was happening in her kingdom, and especially after *seeing* the life Jake had lived over the centuries, I knew it was up to Del and me to change things.

Glancing around my humble abode, I wondered how many weeks would pass before Jake and I returned. He had so much still to show me about his life, our history, and our people. About the world. Years of communities and hideouts, and a better understanding of our lineage if I was going to lead and protect our people when he was gone again. Because Jake was a ghost, and he would leave us again.

Shrugging into my pack, I glanced around the cabin one last time, opened my front door, and stepped out onto the porch where Beast lounged in a splash of sunlight. He took in the sight of me and groaned, laying his head back down in defiance.

"What, are you getting old on me or something?" I said,

shaking my head. "You've had a whole month to relax." His tail whipped caustically and his eyes flitted closed as if he couldn't hear me.

I saw a flit of black feathers from the corner of my eye as I stepped off the porch. Squinting, I strained to see a very familiar, very cantankerous looking raven. My heartbeat thumped double-time, and I smiled. "Well, look what the cat dragged in," I said as Sid landed on a low hanging redwood bough. I opened my mind to Sid's and saw a flutter of images—of the sea and the city and of Del tying a note to his leg.

"A message?" I couldn't suppress my growing grin or whirring pulse.

Spreading his wings, Sid sailed closer, landing on the porch step behind me. Beast eyed the raven closely, flicking his tail farther out of Sid's reach as if the cougar was worried he might get a love peck.

Sid blinked at him, and I bent down to untie the message from his leg. I swallowed thickly as I unrolled it and began to read.

I wanted you to be the first to know - all Healers have been released and returned to their families. And this is only the beginning. -D

P.S. Summer Solstice festival in June? I might know someone who can sneak you in. :)

I stared at the scroll, my thoughts torn between imagining the scowl on the queen's face when she had learned Del was going to free her precious captives, and wondering if two months was enough time for Jake and me to return from our trip before the festival.

As I read Del's note again, I wondered how, exactly, the queen had explained her atrocities to the people. But then I reminded myself all that mattered was that Del had kept her word, and the future of Corvo City would be a better one because of her.

The Summer Solstice. With a grin, I held up the slip of paper. "A personal invite by her royal highness, eh, Sid?" I said, glancing down at the raven. "How could I refuse? Don't go yet."

Dropping my pack on the dirt with a thud, I leapt past Sid and Beast on the porch and hurried back into the cabin.

There were a hundred things I wanted to say to Del, but I held onto them for the festival, when our paths would cross again. Instead, I wrote:

I never doubted you for a minute, tough stuff. -F
    P.S. As you wish, princess.

"Fin!" Jake's voice echoed from outside.

Rolling up the paper, I hurried out the front door again and latched it behind me.

"We're burning daylight, kid!" Jake called from down the dirt walkway. He leaned against a giant redwood, his arms crossed over his chest and his pack resting at his feet.

"Almost ready," I told him and tied my response to the raven's leg. "Thanks, Sid."

The bird tilted his head, blinked at me with a less than enthusiastic caw, then sprung into the air, flapping his onyx wings until he disappeared through the trees.

Beast groaned in relief and laid his head down again, grateful the bird was gone so he could continue his morning nap.

"Secret messages?" Jake mused as I lugged my pack back onto my back.

I couldn't contain a smirk as I headed toward him. "Something like that."

He lifted a skeptical eyebrow. "Do I even want to know?"

"Nope," I said easily, which earned me a deep chuckle. With a sidelong look, I fell into step beside Jake. "Come on, lazybones!" I called to Beast as he reluctantly climbed to his feet. "It's time for another adventure."

THE END

Del and Fin's adventures continue in *The Raven Queen*, the first, full-length book in The Ending Legacy.

Have you read the series that started it all? Follow Jake and his fellow Patrons' lives the first year of the Turn in *After The Ending*, book one of The Ending Series.

A Note from the Authors

We hope you enjoyed reading *World After* as much as we enjoyed writing it! It's the introduction to our newest Ending World series, The Ending Legacy, and a direct continuation of The Ending Series: *World Before*. While we know many Endingers were looking forward to more of Dani and Zoe's journey, this was the story that was inside us, waiting to be told—the newest chapter of The Ending, with new characters and new adventures.

From the moment we sat down to write *After The Ending* in 2012, we pondered what would happen to Jake, a man with regenerative powers who was nearly impossible to kill. Would he die like the others? How long would he live and what would the world be like years into the future? While it was bittersweet to write the passing of our beloved Ending Series friends, meeting Del and Fin, and creating a world unlike any we've written so far, was like a breath of fresh air—new, exciting, and we can't wait to unearth more secrets and put our new friends through the wringer, like the rest.

There are more books to come in The Ending Legacy series, and we can't wait to see where Del and Fin take us next!

ALSO BY THE LINDSEYS

THE ENDING WORLD

THE ENDING LEGACY

World After (Prequel)

The Raven Queen

The Ghost King (2024)

THE ENDING SERIES

After The Ending

Into The Fire

Out Of The Ashes

Before The Dawn

The Ending Beginnings

World Before

SAVAGE NORTH CHRONICLES

(An Ending World series by Lindsey Pogue)

The Darkest Winter

The Longest Night

Midnight Sun

Fading Shadows

Untamed

Unbroken

Day Zero: Beginnings

MORE BOOKS BY LINDSEY POGUE

FORGOTTEN LANDS WORLD

(Can be read as stand-alones)

FORGOTTEN LANDS

Dust and Shadow

Borne of Sand and Scorn Prequel Novella

Earth and Ember

Tide and Tempest

RUINED LANDS

City of Ruin

Sea of Storms

Land of Fury (March 2023)

SARATOGA FALLS LOVE STORIES

(Recommended reading order)

Whatever It Takes

Nothing But Trouble

Told You So

Memory Book Story Collection

For a reading list, trigger warnings, ebooks, audiobooks, and more, visit
www.LindseyPogue.com

OTHER NOVELS BY LINDSEY SPARKS

About Lindsey Pogue

Lindsey Pogue is a genre-bending fiction author, best known for her soul-stirring, post-apocalyptic survival series, Savage North Chronicles and Forgotten Lands. As an avid romance reader with a master's in history and culture, Lindsey's adventures cross genres and push boundaries, weaving together facts, fantasy, and timeless love stories of epic proportions. When Lindsey's not chatting with readers, plotting her next storyline, or dreaming up new, brooding characters, she's wrapped in blankets watching her favorite action flicks with her own leading man. They live in Northern California with their rescue cats, Beast and little girl Blue.

Facebook: Author Lindsey Pogue
Facebook Reader Group: Lindsey Pogue's Reader Group
Instagram: @AuthorLindseyPogue
Bookbub: Lindsey Pogue
Goodreads: Lindsey Pogue
Patreon: Lindsey Pogue
TikTok: @AuthorLindseyPogue
YouTube: Lindsey Pogue
Newsletter: lindseypogue.com/newsletter
www.lindseypogue.com

ABOUT LINDSEY SPARKS

Lindsey Sparks lives her life with one foot in a book—so long as that book transports her to a magical world or bends the rules of science. Her novels, from Post-apocalyptic (writing as Lindsey Fairleigh) to Time Travel Romance, always offer up a hearty dose of unreality, along with plenty of history, intrigue, adventure, and romance.

When she's not working on her next novel, Lindsey spends her time hanging out with her two little boys, working in her garden, or playing board games with her husband. She lives in the Pacific Northwest with her family and their small pack of cats and dogs. www.authorlindseysparks.com

PATREON: https://www.patreon.com/lindseysparks

MAIN SOCIAL MEDIA

FB Reader Group: Lindsey's Lovely Readers
Instagram: @authorlindseysparks
YouTube: Author Lindsey Sparks
Discord: discord.gg/smTeDHQBhT

OTHER SOCIAL MEDIA

Facebook: @authorlindseysparks
TikTok: @authorlindseysparks
Pinterest: @authorlindseysparks

www.authorlindseysparks.com/join-newsletter